FLAMES FOR THE SHEIKH

A NOVEL BY

ANNABELLE WINTERS

FLAMES FOR THE SHEIKH

A NOVEL BY

ANNABELLE WINTERS

2016
RAINSHINE BOOKS
USA

Copyright Notice

FLAMES FOR THE SHEIKH

1

"Jennifer Bethany Jones, MBA. Oh, look at that, all fancy and all! Woo hoo! And this paper is nice too! Thick. Creamy. How much did these cost you?"

"More than I wanted to spend," Jenny said, reaching to take the business card back from her cousin Paula, who was about to slip it into the front pocket of her jeans. "And I only got a hundred made, so I'll take that back, thank you very much."

She took the card back, holding it up and admiring it one more time before putting it back into the stainless steel card holder (which had cost extra). The cards were expensive but damn nice, she had to admit. Beautiful, crisp printing. Heavy-duty card-stock paper. That nice cream color. And, now that she thought about it, adding in her middle name and the "MBA" thing didn't sound too pretentious. Sure, the degree was from City College of Chicago, which wasn't exactly Harvard, and it was a "condensed" MBA that she got part-time (with a bunch of online classes), but it was still an MBA. It looked professional. It sounded professional. And it was important to look and sound professional when you were asking a professional investor to invest in you.

"The fact that you're putting in some of your own money is going to count for a lot," Jenny's entrepreneurship professor had told her when she went to him for advice a year ago, shortly after getting her diploma. "The high-end restaurant business is very tough, Jenny, and any smart investor is going to know that. But they're also going to know that if it's done right, a restaurant can do exceedingly well in a city like Chicago."

"Just have to make sure to do it right, then," Jenny had said cheerfully, even though she was anxious like an umbrella in a lightning storm. "First Chicago, and then the world!"

The professor had raised an eyebrow at this. "The world? You're thinking of building a restaurant chain, Jenny? I thought it was going to be a high-end, classy place."

"It is," Jenny had said. "Eclectic food. A mix of small

plates and gourmet entrées. World-class wine selection. Desserts from heaven. Or hell, maybe, considering the amount of chocolate that'll be in each one. But yes, I want to go high-end, but I also see it expanding into a chain."

The professor sighed, lowering his glasses and looking closely at Jenny, like he was searching her face for something. "Jenny," he said. "It's hard enough to succeed with a high-end restaurant in one location. Luck, timing, marketing—all of it's got to come together. Yes, you have a shot at it, in my opinion. You were one of my best students, and I think you've also got that . . . that spark that I see in some of the best entrepreneurs. That deep faith in yourself, in your vision, in your ability. It's something that's very hard to teach. So yes, you've got a shot at it. I think if anyone can make a go at this, it's you." He paused again. "But turning a single restaurant into a chain . . . well, that's a whole different ballgame. And the fact that it's a high-end, classy place . . . it's tough. Very difficult to grow that sort of brand in the restaurant world. You don't see it much, do you? A burger or sandwich joint can expand into a franchise, but you don't see a high-end French restaurant with thirty locations across five continents. And you know why? Because it's damn near impossible. The marketing is a different game when you go high-end. Damn near impossible."

"Impossible, Prof?" Jenny had said, feeling that spark in her then as she smiled even though the anxiety was rising, that sickening feeling of self-doubt, that maybe she was kidding herself, maybe she should just get a regular job at a big company and think it over for a few years. Graduates from even the top MBA programs were doing that—getting safe jobs with good money and working their way up instead of betting on a new business. Everyone knew that most new businesses failed, usually wiping out all the investors—certainly wiping out the founder. And a failed business isn't great to have on your resume!

The professor had laughed. "All right, you got me. I always tell the class that the most successful entrepreneurs were often told early on that what they were doing was impossible. So all right, Jenny. Send me your business plan when you have the numbers worked out, and I'll take a look and tell you what I think."

"I've already got the numbers worked out," Jenny had said, pulling out her phone and scrolling feverishly. "Sending it right now."

The professor had laughed again, shaking his head. "Why am I not surprised? All right, Jenny. I'll take a look at it as soon as I get a chance."

That was a year ago, and when Jenny didn't hear back from the professor, she was sort of offended but then just shrugged it off and moved on. She had other things to do, securing a space for the restaurant being top of the list. Location, location, location, right? Right.

She had already scouted out a place that was currently vacant. It was a beautiful, circular room with large windows that faced the street. Just off Michigan Avenue in Downtown Chicago, the location couldn't be more perfect. Being off the main drag meant that traffic noise wouldn't be as bad. At the same time, it was so close to some of the best, most exclusive shopping in the world, that she'd get a lot of foot-traffic from people who most certainly had the money to spend. Yes, the space was perfect. So perfect that she considered making the deposit payment right away, out of her own money—the last of her tiny inheritance.

But she held off. She knew it would be an emotional decision to simply plop down all the personal money she had set aside for investing in the restaurant. Yes, that money would eventually go into the business, but her money wouldn't be nearly enough to finance everything—not even for a few months! No, she needed a real investor to throw in with her. Big money. It wasn't going to be easy, and so Jenny knew she couldn't sink all her own money into the security deposit up front. What if it took her six months to find an investor? What if it took a year? What if she never got the big money she needed to kick this thing off? She'd be bankrupt with nothing to show for it! No, she needed to get the outside funding before committing to the place. After all, the rent alone would wipe her out in two months!

Jenny had researched a list of potential investors, and she was ready with her pitch. She had a Power-Point presentation all set. She knew exactly what she'd wear. And those business cards! She was going to rule the *world*! Woo hoo!

So she started reaching out to investors, most of which were small or large venture capital firms based in Chicago and the Midwest. She sent out introductory letters, following up by email and then with phone calls. But soon she found that she could barely get past the administrative assistants—the gatekeepers. And that was her first dose of reality: Sometimes it doesn't matter how good your idea and business plan is, because if you don't get a chance to make your pitch to the people with the money, you're finished before you even get started.

At the eight-month mark, despair started to creep in, but Jenny ignored that sinking feeling and instead kept going, forcing herself to keep smiling as she made yet another phone call to an administrative assistant who politely said, "We'll get back to you if we're interested in hearing more about your proposal, Ms. Jones." Of course, nobody ever got back to her.

And then, as she was getting close to the end of her

list, close to the end of her rope, her patience, maybe her resolve, the email from Bukhaara Private Capital, LLC, showed up in her inbox.

2

It arrived the next evening, while Cousin Paula was over for a late dinner.

Jenny had wanted to cook for Paula, but instead had spent the day trying to work her graduate school network, trying to get a contact at an investment firm. It had been rough, because most of City College's MBA grads either worked at large local companies (which weren't into financing restaurants) or were not particularly helpful.

So it had been a rough day—eight months of rough days, really—and skipping lunch hadn't done her mood any favors. Jenny was tired and hungry, that sinking feeling of despair thick in her gut, and so they had just ordered pizza—her comfort food—from the Italian place down the street. It tasted like the best thing on Earth, Jenny thought as she inhaled the first slice and reached for the second, still chewing, her eyes wide as she realized she hadn't eaten in almost eighteen hours.

"Wow, you are *hungry*, babe," Paula said, eyeing Jenny up and down with affectionate amusement. "I guess the diet's off for today. Not that you need to diet. Hell, I'd kill for those curves!"

Jenny blinked as she swallowed, looking down at the gigantic slice of pizza in her hand, cheese falling off the sides like molten white lava, that puddle of salty grease pooling in the oversized cuts of pepperoni, each of which looked like a mini-pizza on its own. She'd been on a low-carb, low-fat, high-protein diet for three months now, trying to knock off some of those extra pounds she had tacked on from her crazy schedule working part-time jobs and handling part-time classes.

Jenny had always been a curvy woman, but the past two years had really been out of control, she knew. Pizza four nights a week. Junk food at late-night study sessions. Beers at Happy Hour every Thursday with her classmates. At the time she knew she was putting on weight, but with the casual, almost college environment of the classroom sessions, she didn't really care. She wore sweatpants when she was feeling fat, and she was getting asked out on dates enough that it didn't seem like any of the guys minded the extra weight.

Of course, dating hadn't been a priority for Jenny recently—certainly not until she had gotten her degree and started the next phase of her perfectly planned life. This degree would cost most of her savings over two years, and she wasn't going to take her eyes off the ball. Sure, she had that small inheritance, but she needed to save that for the restaurant. And Chicago wasn't cheap. So no, she wasn't going to get distracted by some man-drama, and being the kind of person she was, the all-or-nothing sort of way she approached things, Jenny understood that it meant she'd have to keep her distance from any man she might actually start to like.

Don't even start, she had said when she found herself vaguely liking this sorta cool guy Steve who had been flirting with her with the kind of persistence and determination that was respectful and flattering while still unyielding.

She did go out with him eventually, after one of the Thursday night happy hours when she had put away more than her usual two or three beers. They went out for Irish Coffee and dessert at a late-night café near his apartment building, and the mixture of sugar, caffeine, and whiskey was just enough to get her to say, "Sure," when he invited her upstairs.

They kissed on his couch, and she liked it when he touched her breasts, she liked it when he gasped in ecstasy as he undid her buttons, she liked it when he almost swooned as he took her full breasts in his hands, his fingers teasing her nipples until they stiffened.

She let him take off her shirt, and she stretched out on his couch, arms above her head as he sucked her nipples, kissed her belly, licked her belly-button until she laughed and squealed. And when he undid the button on her jeans, sliding down the zip as he began to push his face in there, taking deep breaths of her sex, she almost let him continue. Almost.

"I'm sorry," she said, pushing his head away as she struggled to sit up. "I really can't do this right now."

"Are you serious," he had said, his eyes wide, the look on his face partly disbelief and partly begging. "You have to be kidding!"

"I'm really, really sorry. I know it's lame of me to let it get to this point and then back off. It's not you. I actually really like you. And you've been cool. I just can't do this right now. I told myself I wouldn't. I just had a few too many tonight, and—"

"You are *kidding*!" he shouted, straddling her and looking up at the ceiling in frustration. But then he sighed and backed off. "Oh, man! I was so . . . so looking forward to . . ."

Jenny struggled to sit up and find her clothes. She

could feel the folds on her stomach bunching up as she sat, and she quickly put her bra back on as she felt the arousal leave her.

Yeah, she did sorta like him, she thought as she gave him one last apologetic look before heading out the door as a sense of relief washed over her. But she also knew she was a bit drunk and, well, it had been a while since she had gone this far with anyone, so she wasn't sure she could trust her judgment. Sex was a great and wonderful thing, Jenny thought, but although she wasn't the judgmental type, she had never been much for going to bed with a man unless they were in a relationship, unless it was more than just, "I sorta like him."

No, sex outside a relationship had never been Jenny's thing, even though she didn't judge any of her girlfriends for doing it. If anything, her friends would judge her for being too much of a prude! Even Grandma agreed with them sometimes!

Oh, God, didn't Grandma tell me I had a great "baby bucket" or something once? Jenny had thought that night as she took the elevator down alone, checking herself in the mirror as she straightened her top and patted her curves.

"Honey, you've got the most beautiful birthing hips," Jenny said to herself in her best imitation of her late grandmother, who had almost raised her single-handedly, with Jenny's parents seemingly always at work or otherwise engaged. Grandma would say that every time she sensed Jenny was feeling a bit down or self-conscious about her curves. "A real man will never be able to resist those womanly hips of yours, little Jenny. You remember that. A real man won't be able to keep away."

Jenny laughed at the memory, and by the time she walked out of the apartment building and onto the busy sidewalks of downtown Chicago, she was feeling sober and right, confident and strong. I made the right choice there, she told herself. I have to stick to my path and trust that I'll find my man along the way. Right now, getting involved with someone could take me off my path. Even worse, I could get pulled into walking HIS path—whoever he is. Nope. Not happening again. No freaking way.

But that was over a year ago, when she was several pounds lighter, and now she looked up at Paula and then down at that slice of pizza and suddenly she thought she could feel spare tires around her belly, folds along her sides, faint ripples along her thighs. What have I given up, she wondered as she thought of that guy Steve and the others that she had let pass by. Where am I now, compared to before graduate school? I'm older, poorer, fatter, and more alone! All the time I've spent planning this restaurant crap is looking like it was a waste. I'm never going to get the funding I need—not in time, anyway. I'll have to scramble to get a real job, because I skipped out on the on-campus interviews and now all the decent companies have already hired their quotas for the year. And I've been basically unemployed for eight months already. So I'll waste a year because . . . because . . . because I decided to bet on myself instead of some big corporation? Oh, my God! What have I done? What have I done!

Jenny tossed the half-eaten piece of pizza back into her plate and looked up at Paula. Oh, God, I'm going to cry, Jenny thought as she felt everything come to a head in a ball of emotion. All the stress of choosing to stay unemployed while she worked on her business plan. All the frustration of not getting a chance to present her proposal to even one solitary investor. The fear that she had found the ideal space for the restaurant, but might lose it because she didn't have an investor lined up yet. And she was alone. And fat. Oh, God, I'm gonna cry.

"Jenny?" Paula said, her face turning a distinctly paler shade as she dropped her own slice of pizza and grabbed Jenny by the wrist. "You OK? You look like you're about to pass out."

"I just . . . need to go to the bathroom," Jenny said, the words coming out one by one, slowly, each syllable requiring an extraordinary degree of effort to pronounce as she tried to hold back a flood of tears that seemed to want to come for no reason and for every reason.

She stood up slowly, pizza crumbs falling off her boobs as they jiggled beneath her green t-shirt, a piece of crust bouncing down her black sweatpants. She stared down at Paula, who was sprawled on the carpet along with the pizza. Then she turned toward the bathroom, wondering if the door was thick enough so Paula wouldn't hear her cry.

You are not going to cry, she told herself as she took a step toward the bathroom, and suddenly it was Grandma's voice in her head. You are not a child. You don't get to throw a tantrum the moment things don't go your way. How are you going to manage a restaurant? How are you going to manage a business of restaurants? How are you going to handle yourself if an investor says no to your face? Are you going to cry? Are you going to say that your life is hard and you need a break? Hell, no! You've already gotten your lucky break! You finished your MBA! That's a serious degree! It took effort and focus and hard work! You are smart, strong, and powerful! You made it through a grueling two years, just like you said you would! You sacrificed and you persevered! You're not going to crack now! You're so close, honey! Come on, Jenny! Come on, Jennifer Bethany Jones, MBA! Hang on! Just hang on!

And the tears rolled themselves back, and now Jenny could feel her self-confidence rise again, slowly but surely, like water filling a container, filling every corner, leaving no part of her untouched. She had that spark, right? That "unteachable" faith in herself. Well, now's when she needed it, she told herself. Now, goddamn it!

And as if in response, that spark made itself known deep inside her as she felt herself smile with relief as she remembered that she *loved* herself, that she *loved* her body, that she *loved* life and everything that came with it! Finally she slowly turned back to Paula, who was still staring up at her, still not sure what the hell was going on.

"Sorry," Jenny said. "I just had a . . . moment."

Paula gave her the most wide-eyed look ever. "You mean like a senior moment? Like Grandma had before she took off all her clothes and walked out the front door that night?"

Jenny burst out laughing, joining Paula on the floor again, feeling only slightly crazy now. "Something like that, yeah, Paula. Thanks." She picked up her slice of pizza. "Though I'm pretty sure Grandma was just straight-up drunk that time."

Paula rolled over onto her back with laughter, and now the two of them were laughing together, and it was only when they were done with the pizza and the Grandma jokes that Jenny noticed the "New Message" alert flashing on her phone.

And there it was, as if the universe had been watching Jenny overcome her crisis of confidence, as if the universe approved of how Jenny talked herself back onto her own path, as if the universe was sending a little help her way, to keep her on that path. Because there it was: the message from Bukhaara Private Capital, inviting Jenny to come into their Webster Street offices to discuss her business proposal with the general partner, Ms. Yasmeena Bukhaara.

And when Jenny saw the message, she couldn't help but think of what Grandma used to say often: The universe likes to help everyone, but most of all the universe likes to help those who help themselves. So when things are bad and it feels like you can't hold on, if you grit your teeth and hold on just a little while longer, the universe will send help in the strangest of ways.

3

"I would like to help you, Ms. Jones. Ms. Jones? I do not like that. Too generic American. What is your full name? OK, I see it on this cheap business card. Jennifer Bethany Jones? Jennifer Bethany? Why two first names?" The man thought for a moment, his dark eyes flashing mischief as he glanced up from Jenny's "cheap" business card. He pursed his full, dark red lips, rubbed the deep brown stubble on his chin. "I like the name Bethany—it is unusual—to me at least. But it is a longer name than Jenny, and I do not know you well enough to decide whether you are worth the extra effort of speaking an extra syllable every time I address you. So you are Jenny. Jenny, yes? Jenny Jones. Yes, that sounds very American. Perfectly American. Jenny Jones from Chicago. I like it." The man tossed the card onto the massive wooden desk and stood up from his leather chair.

The man stood tall, his broad frame towering above the imposingly large desk, its thick dark wood shining in the hard yellow light of the sprawling office. He was handsome, no doubt, Jenny thought as she glanced up into his eyes, doing a double-take when she saw they were a deep green, the color so dark it was almost black. His hair was thick and dark brown, impeccably styled, and even his three-day stubble looked like it had been trimmed by a professional. He wore perfectly fitted black pinstriped trousers, a tailored, blindingly white shirt with three buttons undone, no undershirt, the median of a sculpted chest and the top of what appeared to be a ridiculously cut six-pack clearly visible.

He had looked right at her breasts when she walked in, his gaze shamelessly taking in their swell before moving down along the curves of her wide hips, the contours of her shapely legs. He didn't stare long enough to make her uncomfortable, though, and when he looked into her eyes and shook her hand, Jenny couldn't deny that the tingle she felt wasn't just pre-meeting nerves.

The man hadn't introduced himself, and there had

been no name on the solid oak door. There was no nameplate on the desk either. So Jenny looked into his eyes and took a breath and said, "I'm sorry. I didn't catch your name. The email I got said I'd be meeting with Ms. Yasmeena Bukhaara?"

"I'm Kabeer Bukhaara," the man said as he sat down smoothly on his dark red leather chair behind that tremendously thick and wide desk. He pushed back from the desk and leaned back and smiled, and there was that tingle again running through Jenny. He gestured towards one of the upright chairs across from him, motioning for Jenny to sit. "Yasmeena is my sister, though she believes she is my mother sometimes. You do not know who I am?"

Jenny blinked, inhaling sharply and blinking again—like five times. The name was familiar, and oh, God, of *course* she knew who he was—by reputation, at least! His name often came up in the local gossip columns that Paula would obsessively read and equally obsessively describe to Jenny, giving her unwanted (but interesting) updates on who was seen where, with whom, and all the rumors that went along with that. Certainly the name of Kabeer Bukhaara came up now and then, mostly because . . . because . . . well, because he was a *prince*! Yes, Kabeer was the billionaire son of a billionaire Middle-Eastern Sheikh, and had chosen to live in Chicago, where he seemed to do a lot of interesting things with interesting people. He was also very, very photogenic.

And now Jenny remembered Paula holding up her phone to show off some of the photographs: Kabeer Bukhaara surfing in Hawaii; Kabeer Bukhaara swimming in St. Bart's; Kabeer Bukhaara sunbathing in Brazil . . . naked!

Ohmygod, I've seen his ass! she thought suddenly in a panic at that memory of Paula showing her a broad-shouldered man from behind, naked and tanned bronze, muscles weaved across his shoulders and arms, buttocks toned and perfect under the Rio de Janeiro sun.

"Um, OK, yes, of course I've heard of you," Jenny said, the blood rushing to her face and then rushing down equally fast, making her feel faint. She blinked and tried to get that image out of her mind, but it wouldn't go, and now she was looking at his chest, her eyes trailing downwards, and . . . oh, thank God he was sitting down, that heavy desk covering most of him. "But I didn't . . ." she stammered.

"Didn't recognize me with my clothes on?" he said, smiling wide, his green eyes sparkling as he made the sort of eye contact that almost made Jenny feel dirty. "I get that a lot. What can I say? Maybe I just have the kind of face that people forget."

"Or maybe people just remember other things about you," Jenny said without thinking, and now she turned bright red when she realized what he might take that to mean. Then she wondered what the hell she actually did mean by that, and she was mortified, petrified, stupefied. "Oh, *God*," she gushed, her life flashing before her eyes now that she remembered she was in a business meeting. "That's not what I meant, Mr. Bukhaara."

But Kabeer Bukhaara was laughing, his head tilting back, lean body rocking back and forth in his leather swivel chair, his perfect white teeth on display, eyes squinting with amusement but still focused on her. "Ah, that was excellent! And call me Kabeer, please. Mr. Bukhaara is my dad. Nobody calls me Mr. Bukhaara."

"Really?" Jenny said, not sure where the confidence to keep speaking was coming from. "So what does your butler call you?"

"My *butler*? Haha! Well then, Miss Jenny. What does *your* butler call *you*?"

Jenny laughed spontaneously. "Well, I'm not a billionaire *Sheikh* with a penthouse in Chicago's Gold Coast, a mansion in Lake Forest, a summer estate in the Florida Keys, and what I assume is a *palace* in your nation-state of Bukhaara!" She shrugged in a way that felt almost flirtatious, but she couldn't help herself. "But if I *were* all those things, then I would most *certainly* have a butler! And his name would be—"

"So wait, you *do* know something about me then," Kabeer said, interrupting and leaning forward, elbows on the desk, eyes focused and alert now. "What else do you know about me?"

Jenny felt those butterflies again now, and her face

was flush, her heat rising. "Well, uh, that you studied law but never passed the bar exam—"

"Actually, I never *took* the bar exam. There is a difference. You make it sound like I failed it. I do not fail."

"Oh, yeah, right. That's what I meant. I mean, I'm just telling you what I've heard from people—mostly my cousin Paula. I mean, I never . . ."

"Never checked my Wikipedia page?"

Jenny blinked. "Well, no. You have a Wikipedia page?"

Kabeer pulled out his iPhone and tapped on it. Just one tap. "Here," he said, handing the phone to Jenny.

It was opened to his Wikipedia page, and Jenny wondered for a moment if she was actually expected to read it right then.

"Yes, go on. Read it," Kabeer said, leaning back and placing his feet on the desk, crossing one leg over the other, his Italian shoes scuffing the smooth teakwood polish.

"Right now?"

"Correct. Right now."

"Uh, OK." Jenny did an internal eye roll and began to read. Some of it she already knew, she realized: high school at Eton in Great Britain, undergrad at Paris-Sorbonne University (graduated ninth in his class; internationally ranked in squash); law school at Columbia (made it to law review). All kinds of achievements ranging from archery contest wins to open-water diving certifications and martial arts black belts (aikido and jujitsu). A section on the various celebrity women linked to him over the years (models, movie stars, billionaire heiresses, even a European princess). And then a section on a handful of arrests and citations, mostly for disorderly conduct, breaking and entering, and one that looked more serious: a recent arrest for assault and battery.

"Wait," Jenny said as she noticed something odd on the page. "Is this in Edit mode? Are you actually updating your own Wikipedia page right now?"

Kabeer shrugged and leaned forward, hands with palms upturned, green eyes looking sweet and innocent beyond belief. "Well, I had to set the record straight, my dear Jenny! Those assault and battery charges are rubbish! I should know—I'm a bloody lawyer!"

"Not if you didn't pass the bar exam. Oh, excuse me—didn't *take* the bar exam," Jenny retorted, feeling her own smile break through as Kabeer laughed in delight at her quip.

Then Kabeer pointed at the phone again, and Jenny blinked and went back to the Wikipedia page. She clicked on a link, which took her to the original news article. There was a clear picture of Kabeer, shirtless and looking lean and ripped, throwing a punch at a man who seemed to be the size of a truck. There was another picture of Kabeer's fist connecting with the man's jaw, every muscle in Kabeer's arm flexed and tight. And finally, there was a picture of the man going down, his eyes closed, like he was out cold on his feet from Kabeer's blow, unconscious before he even hit the ground.

"Um," Jenny said. "Well, I'm not a lawyer. But that man certainly appears to be getting battered by someone who looks sorta like you, Mr. Bukhaara."

"I told you to call me Kabeer. And yes, I'm not saying I did not punch the asshole. Yes, I hit him. And the other man too—that one is not on film—thank God. But those guys assaulted me outside that club! And I was with a woman, so I did not want to take any chances. With two attackers, you must make sure that your first few punches count. You must put the first man down hard—unconscious if possible. You do not want him getting up to help his friend, you know?"

"Of course," Jenny said, blinking hard, not sure what to think. She was silent for a moment, and then realized she was still staring at that shirtless photograph of Kabeer, his jaw set tight, muscles in his arms and torso shining with sweat, his eyes focused and determined, his balance perfect as he landed that blow, his follow-through after the punch making it look like he had done this before. Also in the photograph was a woman who looked familiar, like Jenny had seen her on a billboard or a full-page ad in some magazine. The woman in the picture wasn't looking at the large man who was going down. No, she was staring at Kabeer, a look of pure adulation on her face. Jenny took a moment to look at the woman:

high cheekbones, sunken hollows instead of actual cheeks, twiggy body that looked like it hadn't hit puberty yet, even though the woman was clearly in her twenties. That's your type, huh, Kabeer? she thought as she suddenly felt a wave of self-consciousness go through her as she pulled at the bottom of her suit jacket, which felt uncomfortably tight right then.

The feeling woke her up a bit, throwing a dose of reality back into the situation. What the hell are you doing, Jenny, she asked herself. This is the biggest business meeting of your life. It's not a goddamn first date! What the hell is *wrong* with you, girl? Why do you even *care* what this billionaire Sheikh's type is?

She was about to hand the phone back to Kabeer when it suddenly vibrated in her hand. A text message notification popped up on the screen:

Yasmeena: Where are you Kabeer? Father is waiting and he is angry. And I am even more angry.

Jenny quickly put the phone on the desk and slid it over to Kabeer. He didn't reach for it.

"I think you just got a message," Jenny said, pointing at the phone.

Kabeer shrugged. "Anything important?"

What am I, your secretary? Jenny thought, but she just shrugged like she hadn't read the message.

Kabeer smirked, his eyes still focused on Jenny. "OK, Jenny, if the phone vibrated in your hand, then the message must have popped up on the screen, and you must have at least looked at it." He laughed, a

cocky I-am-so-comfortable-with-my-awesomeness-
and-power-that-I-don't-care-if-anyone-reads-my-
private-messages look on his handsome, naturally
tanned face. "So just tell me who it is from."

Jenny swallowed once and looked him in the eye.
"Yasmeena. She wants to know where you are. I
guess your dad's waiting, and he's pissed. They're
both pissed."

And now Kabeer's expression changed, a bit of that
natural tan appearing to fade as he went pale and
grabbed the phone. "Ya, Allah," he muttered under
his breath as he began to furiously type. He tapped
once and waited. A few seconds later a message came
back in, and he exhaled.

He looked up at her, a wry smile curling his lips that
looked very clean and full, now that Jenny glanced
at his mouth. I bet he's a great kisser, she thought,
as she tried to remember the last time she'd kissed
someone. Maybe that guy Steve. Was that seriously
the last time? Holy smokes, that was over a year ago!
She glanced at Kabeer's lips once again. When was the
last time a woman kissed those lips, she wondered,
allowing herself to drift for a moment as Kabeer focused on his phone again.

Now Kabeer stood up, turning around and reaching
for his jacket, which was draped over a chair off to the
side. As he turned his back to her, Jenny remembered
that photograph again, the one of him on the beach
in Rio, sun beating down on his bare back, naked but-

tcheeks, muscular legs. Did she remember seeing the edges of a tattoo around the meaty part of his right arm? Oh, hell, will you get a grip, Jenny! Jeez.

"Come on," Kabeer said now, putting his jacket on and beckoning to Jenny with a head motion directed towards the door. "Let us ride."

"Ride?" Jenny said, not sure what was happening but standing up anyway, straightening her black skirt and carefully navigating her heels through the treacherously deep carpet that seemed to change color from dark maroon to shining purple as she walked. "Where are we going?"

"The lake," Kabeer said, striding to the thick wooden door and holding it open for Jenny, who was trying to hurry without falling on her face.

"Lake?"

"Lake Michigan," Kabeer said with a laugh as he put his arm around Jenny's waist for a moment to usher her out as the door fell shut behind her. He leaned in close, so close she could smell his subtle cologne—a hint of tobacco leaf, she thought—very masculine. "You know, that big lake near downtown?" His arm tightened around her waist as he led her out, and as they turned the corner, she felt him pull her close and lean in again as he finished the sentence.

"Yes, I know Lake Michigan," Jenny said with a nervous laugh. She was vividly aware of his arm around her waist, and even more vividly aware of the looks she was getting from the few other employees—mostly young women with bodies by Chanel. They glanced at her, then at Kabeer, and then back at her. For a moment she felt a wave of indignation that Kabeer thought it was appropriate to touch her that way at a business meeting. But she had to admit that it felt all right. Felt nice even. There was an electricity there, she thought, when he touched her. And the way his strong arm circled her waist so easily . . . the way his fingers tightened against her side as he guided her into the elevator . . . the way she felt her heat rise, her heart beat, her stomach flutter . . . yes, it was all right. It was all right.

"Why Lake Michigan?" Jenny asked as the elevator doors opened in the downstairs lobby.

"That's where the yacht is," Kabeer said, his arm tightening around her waist again as he guided her towards a different set of elevators. "This way. We're parked underground."

"Yacht?" Jenny said, feeling like a parrot or something as she shuffled her heels into the second elevator.

Kabeer turned to her and smiled, clearly aware of— and clearly pleased with—the effect he was having on her. "Yes. One of our yachts. I forgot that Yasmeena and I had a meeting with Father this afternoon. He is visiting America to check on his businesses."

"Oh," Jenny said, looking down at her heels. "Well, of course, we can reschedule. I mean—"

"Absolutely not. You're coming with me." Kabeer

stepped out of the elevator, pulling Jenny with him, his arm still firmly around her waist. The elevator doors closed behind them, and Jenny realized they were in an underground garage that was very large, very empty, and rather alarmingly private. Kabeer pointed towards the left. "That's us."

Jenny looked over and saw three BMW stretch limousines. They seemed unmanned and silent. "I don't see any drivers," she said.

Kabeer looked at her with a frown. Then he tilted his head back and let out a clear, delighted laugh. "Oh, no. We are not taking one of those monster-sized limos! That is my ride over there, behind the third car."

Jenny squinted into the darkness, and finally she made out the silhouette of a motorcycle. It was large, heavy, and black. It looked absolutely terrifying, especially since she was in a narrow, knee-length skirt and heels.

"No way," she said, almost laughing at the absurdity of putting her round ass on the back of that thing. "Absolutely not."

"Absolutely yes," Kabeer said. "It is the only way we are getting through downtown traffic in time. I have got an extra helmet. Come, Jenny. It will actually be fun. The helmets have headsets, so we can even talk while we ride."

"You don't get it," Jenny said, shutting down completely as she stopped dead in her tracks. The motorcycle looked even more intimidating now that she saw it up close. And the backseat looked incredibly high up off the ground—how the hell was she supposed to even climb on there? "I'm wearing heels. Um . . . and a skirt."

Kabeer looked at her feet, his eyes traveling up her legs, taking in the sight of her full hips once again. Now he looked back down at her legs and shrugged. "The heels can stay here. We'll get you some of Yasmeena's shoes on board. As for the skirt . . ." he grinned now, those green eyes twinkling even in the blue-tinted darkness of the private underground garage. Kabeer came close now, so close that in a panic Jenny thought ohmygod he's going to kiss me, right here! She inhaled sharply as she smelled his musk, sensed his heat, took in his aura. The silence was deafening, and Jenny shivered and felt her tongue dart out involuntarily as Kabeer slowly, subtly, smoothly traced his finger down the small of her back. It was so inappropriate, Jenny thought. So not done. So wrong. So . . . so . . . oh, God . . .

"Kabeer," she whispered, her eyelids fluttering as she focused on his singular touch that was somehow, someway turning her inside out.

"Like I was saying," Kabeer said, his voice low and deep, his breath hot against her cheek. "As for the skirt . . . well, you are wearing tights underneath, yes?"

Jenny blinked. "Well, yeah, but . . ."

"But nothing. What, you have a run in your stocking? A tear in your tights? Here, let me see."

And then slowly but without hesitation, gently but without an invitation, intentionally but without asking, Kabeer went down to his knees in front of Jenny, his hands on her hips, now her sides, and as she gasped and shuddered under his firm touch, the Sheikh ran his hands down along her sides, down the contours of her hips, down along her thick thighs, his fingers curling under the hem of her skirt, hands sliding smoothly up beneath the thick cloth.

She should have pushed him away and screamed for help, she knew. She should have kicked at him, cursed at him, asked him what the hell gave him the right to touch her like that. But she did none of those things, and she couldn't understand why. She wasn't frozen with fear. She wasn't afraid to say no. She wasn't shocked into silence.

No. She was turned on, she realized. Turned on like hell. And now she felt her breath catch as she looked down at this handsome man on his knees before her, his thousand-dollar pants touching the tarmac, and she inhaled deep as she felt his strong hands slide up beneath her skirt, his fingers pressing firmly against her calves, her thighs, now her round bottom as she shivered and gasped.

He ran his fingers along every inch of her broad behind, circling round to the front, his thumb grazing her sex for less than a moment, the touch so subtle that it was almost imperceptible except to the deepest part of her. Now he caressed the front of her thighs, slowly pushing his hand between her legs that were closed tight together because of the skirt.

"I am not finished," he whispered, his face down by her waist, the words spoken quick and clear, almost like a command. He looked up at her now, and she almost melted when she saw the look of desire on his face, a look that told her he was as hot for her as she was for him suddenly. "Come, Jenny," he said again, his green eyes sparkling in a way that was making Jenny dizzy as she felt the Sheikh's rough hand push right where her thighs were pressed together. "Come," he said again, his voice so low and deep that she could feel the sound vibrate inside her. "Let me."

With a deep, shuddering breath Jenny moved her left leg out, allowing Kabeer to slide his hand up between her legs, and she gasped as she felt him against the smooth Spandex of her black tights, so close to her most secret of spaces. She closed her eyes and whimpered, a quivering smile breaking as she pushed away that annoying voice that was screaming "What the *hell* are you doing, Jenny? Are you *insane*?!"

Yes, she closed her eyes and smiled, moving her right leg out now as she spread a little more, spread for him. But then suddenly his touch was gone, and now Kabeer was on his feet, towering above her at full height, and he was looking down at her with that innocent, schoolboy-sexy glint in his eyes, and he said:

"Well, it does not seem like there are any rips or tears in your stockings. So we should be good to go. Just kick off those heels, hike up your skirt, and let us ride, shall we? Come on."

He grinned as Jenny opened her eyes and looked up at him. She looked at his lips, the way his mouth was twisted in a devilish smile, the way his tongue darted out for a moment like the goddamn snake of temptation that he was. Jenny's mouth was hanging open too, but it wasn't a smile on her lips. No, it was an expression of desire, and maybe because it had been so long since she had allowed a man to touch her, she was losing her mind, spiraling out of control.

Still, she couldn't deny what she felt, and with a final internal message to that voice of common sense to shut the hell up and leave her alone, she looked up and stared like she was in a dream as Kabeer leaned in and kissed her.

He kissed her full, his clean, warm lips smothering hers as he pulled her into him, his broad frame easily taking her weight as she felt herself stumble on those heels and lean heavy against him. She kissed him back, opening her mouth wide and letting him in, feeling the warmth of his lips, the heat of his tongue, the depth of his passion as she felt her own depths stir in response.

What she was feeling scared her, and as she felt his hands on the small of her back, slowly moving down along the arched curves of her backside, she knew that her body was opening up in a way she hadn't felt in years, her need rising to a level where she wanted his hands up her skirt again, pushing down inside the back of her tights, grasping at the bare flesh of her bottom, lifting her and pushing her against one of those sleek black limousines, hiking up her skirt as he pushed her legs apart, his muscular hips holding her against the cold metal car door as he unbuckled and unzipped, and—

"We should stop," he whispered now, breaking out of the kiss with a gasp, his open mouth moving down and kissing her chin, her smooth neck, licking her, tasting her, marking her as he circled round to just beneath her ear, finally moving back to her mouth again and giving her a full, deep kiss that send a tremor of heat back through Jenny's shaking body.

She could feel his hardness against her as they kissed—it was unmistakable, almost unbelievable. And now she looked into his eyes again, her tongue hanging out as she shook her head in wonder—wonder at what the hell was going on, at how the hell she had walked into this building planning to pitch a business idea to Yasmeena Bukhaara and was now in a private underground garage, in the arms of her younger brother, billionaire Sheikh Kabeer Bukhaara.

"We need to stop," he said again, his whisper coming out urgent and sharp. "Or else I am not going to be able to stop, Jenny. I don't know what came over me, but I want you. Now. Badly. Your curves are unlike anything I've ever seen. Like damned *nothing* I've ever touched. And your lips, the way you kiss, you're heating me up something wild, getting me so bloody hard, Jenny. I just want to push you up against that car, rip that tight skirt off your magnificent hips, tear those sexy black tights right down the middle, push your panties off to the side and just—"

And he pushed her away and stepped back quickly, shaking his head like a madman. He *shouted* out loud now, looking up at the black ceiling and cursing, and now he turned to one of those black limousines and *rammed* his fist down onto the broad hood of the car, the sound echoing through the empty garage, bouncing off the walls.

"Ya, Allah!" he shouted, his voice echoing out now, the sound coming back in waves. "God *dammit!*"

Jenny just stood there, gently swaying in her heels, her breathing still heavy and labored, her wetness unmistakable now. She watched as Kabeer paced back and forth for a moment, clenching his fists, his entire body tensed up. He seemed to be talking to himself, muttering out loud, oblivious to Jenny. Then he abruptly stopped pacing, turned towards her, that devilish smile on his lips again as his tongue darted out once more.

What the hell, Jenny asked herself as she watched

this incredibly sexy man start to walk towards her, shaking his head like he was talking to himself internally. Is this guy seriously unhinged? Really insane? Cousin Paula had mentioned something a few months ago when she was reading about Kabeer Bukhaara online. Something about serious behavioral problems when he was younger—fighting, refusal to submit to authority. What had Jenny said to Paula back then, sort of flippantly . . . yes, she had said something like, "Well, Paula, if he's a hot billionaire playboy, then all those things are actually qualifications, not faults, yeah?"

Paula had laughed and pretended to swoon as she pulled up that naked-butt photo—that was the first (and only!) time Jenny had seen the picture. But now, she thought, yes now that you're alone in a dark basement with this man—in *his* dark basement, nonetheless—is it as funny, Jenny?

And now she thought back to the way Kabeer had literally *felt her up* as she stood there like a helpless damsel and f-ing *let him*! Oh, my *God*, why didn't I scream and run for help! Why didn't I?

Is it because deep down I know I need this man, need his approval, need his goddamn *money*?! Am I now a *whore*? Or on my way there? Is that all it takes, Jenny? Is this dream so important, so big, so all-encompassing that you're willing to give up your dignity just for a chance at it?

Shivering, angry at herself, questioning her own motives, doubting the legitimacy of her strange attraction to him, Jenny watched Kabeer Bukhaara as he came close and stopped beside one of those black BMWs and leaned against it in his tailored pinstripe trousers, his white shirt that looked just a bit rumpled now. He had calmed down, and his face exuded supreme control, his stance oozing confidence as he gently tapped on the shining metal hood of the long dark limousine, his dark green eyes somehow flashing in the dim lights of the underground world surrounding them.

For a moment it struck Jenny that maybe all that shouting and raging and muttering and punching metal car-doors was an act, part of this man's made-up persona. Perhaps it was an act that he had been doing so long that it was habit now. Habit, but still not real.

Stop it, Jenny. You don't know much about him. Really, you don't know anything at all. Stop trying to make excuses for him in your own freaking mind! Why are you doing that? Why?

Because although I don't know anything about him, she told herself as she watched Kabeer Bukhaara knock twice on that hard black metal of the BMW and then straighten up to full height as he faced her, shamelessly looking at her up and down, taking in her curves, her cups, her contours . . .

Yes, she thought, although I don't know shit about this billionaire Sheikh who is from some far-off Arabian country but for some reason hangs out in Chicago and acts like an American, I do know something about myself: I'm attracted to him. I was turned on by him. And although he didn't ask permission, he touched my body because he sensed that I wouldn't say no.

So now those conflicting thoughts came tearing back into her overloaded brain: So I'm attracted to him but I also need him for my business. How do I navigate this? How the *hell* do I navigate this?

And now Kabeer Bukhaara was close, so close, and she could smell him, feel his heat, literally *taste* his arousal as she saw the look in his eye and realized that her body was reacting to him, opening up for him, welcoming him . . .

But in a moment of total control that seemed to come out of nowhere and everywhere, Jenny looked calmly into Kabeer's blazing green eyes, smiled her own devilish little smile, kicked off her shoes, and walked to that motorcycle.

"OK," she said, her voice almost betraying the effort she was making to do what she was about to do. "Let's ride, Cowboy."

And with a deep breath and a brief moment where she closed her eyes to summon up the courage to do it, she hiked her skirt up over her round hips and stepped right up to the motorcycle, turning as she touched the leather seat, looking back over her shoulder at Kabeer, who was standing dumbstruck. He glanced at her bottom, exposed in her thick black tights, and Jenny could see his breath catch as a deep shudder betrayed his arousal. For a moment Jenny wondered if Kabeer, this billionaire Arab who wasn't used to women turning him down, would be able to pull back from what he had clearly decided he wanted. But the Sheikh looked into her eyes, saw the way she was smiling at him, and slowly began to shake his head.

Then Kabeer Bukhaara came close to her, his chest still heaving, his arousal still awesomely apparent, and he placed his hand on her hip for a moment, leaned in, and said, "OK, you have my attention now, Jenny Jones. My full goddamn attention."

4

Kabeer could feel her weight pushed against him as he downshifted and took a quick left, accelerating as the motorcycle banked hard, forcing Jenny to cling to him. She tightened her grip around his waist now as he sped up again, and when Kabeer got up to cruising speed on the long straight stretch, he felt Jenny rest her cheek against his back. It felt nice, he thought. Why does it feel nice? I've had a lot of different women ride with me, hold me tight, snuggle up like it means something. But it never means something. It's never felt this way. What is different? Ya, Allah, what is different?

It's because she made me stop even though she wanted it, isn't it, Kabeer finally admitted as he felt that lingering arousal turn into a spark of anger, but anger that quickly faded into a tight smile as he thought of how she looked at him when she hiked up her skirt and kicked off her shoes. It took effort and courage to do that, he could tell. God, this woman had the strangest, most endearing mix of self-confidence and self-consciousness, and it struck him as so real, so genuine, so . . . her! In a way Kabeer felt that in less than an hour he knew more about the kind of person Jenny was than he did about that woman he had spent the entire previous summer with! He could barely remember that other woman's name, and already he knew that no matter what, Jenny Jones was a name he'd never forget.

"You are all right?" he said, turning his head halfway and shouting over his shoulder.

Jenny didn't reply, but Kabeer could feel her head move against his back like she was nodding, and her arms tightened around his hard stomach as he tilted his head back and laughed.

"Sorry," he shouted over the roar of the wind. "I forgot the helmets. I guess my mind was elsewhere."

But she didn't reply, and they weaved through traffic together, Jenny hanging on tight as Kabeer gunned the engine, smiling all the way because he felt so damned good for some reason, so bloody great to be riding through town with this courageous, curvaceous, shoeless woman in a hiked-up skirt-suit clinging to him like . . . like . . . like it meant something.

And now Kabeer felt true joy as he roared through the streets of downtown Chicago, hitting Lakeshore Drive at high speed and enjoying the looks the two of them were getting from cyclists, roller-bladers, and stuffy people in their air-conditioned Range Rovers. He felt like a king for moment, riding his chariot through the streets of Bukhaara, his queen by his side, and as Kabeer squinted into the wind and glanced over to the side, he could swear that the tall highrises of downtown Chicago looked like the towering minarets of Bukhaara, and as he blinked and turned the other way, towards Lake Michigan, all that blue was shining like gold sand in the sun, the waves turning into the rolling dunes of that desert, the sailboats reborn as palm trees surrounding one of the three major oases around which Kabeer's ancestors had built the old city of Bukhaara.

A sudden wave of what he could only describe as a deep yearning flooded his being as he became aware once more of the woman pressed up against him, this American woman who had literally just walked into his life and was making him think about things he didn't want to think about: his homeland, his future, the responsibilities he was shrugging off . . . the responsibilities of a leader, a ruler, a king.

The responsibilities of a Sheikh.

Now darkness took over and Kabeer's jaw went tight and his body tensed up and he gunned the engine into a tight turn as he felt Jenny's fingernails dig into him, her face pushing tight into his back. Her physical presence was overwhelming to him suddenly as he focused on how close her soft body felt to his, how her curves seemed to fit just right with his contours, her smoothness the perfect offset to his sharpness. And just like that he was happy again, that darkness buried back down where it wouldn't bother him until he needed to deal with it. Yes, he was happy, and it feel *damned* good to have this sexy, shapely woman clinging to him. And, ya Allah, she was enjoying it too, was she not!

One last turn and he was on the home stretch to the family's private jetty on Lake Michigan, and he banked hard, released the throttle, and finally screeched to a halt on the heavy wooden planks, blue waters to the left and right, a forty-foot yacht blocking out the sky at the end of the dock.

Smiling and nodding, Kabeer tried to dismount, and only then did he realize that Jenny was frozen stiff, like she was scared out of her mind, her arms wrapped around him, her body pressed so tight against his that Kabeer wondered if they'd need to be surgically separated.

"Hey," he said, putting the bike on its stand but

staying seated, laughing a little when Jenny barely moved. "You can let go now. If you want. No hurry."

Jenny took a moment, but slowly she peeled herself off him and managed to step off the bike, quickly pushing her skirt down over her tights, covering her hips. Kabeer got off and turned to her, and he blinked when he saw she was bright red, like a tomato, a beetroot, strawberry pie.

"What's the matter?" he said, reaching out and grabbing her arm.

But she pulled her arm away and covered her face for a moment. "I can't believe I just did that," she said, the words coming out hoarse, her voice wavering, like she was just learning how to speak again.

"Oh, come now," Kabeer said, his voice soft, his eyes looking into hers as he drew close. "Sometimes there's just an attraction that cannot be denied. That will not be denied. No matter what you think of me, I do not take every woman to my private garage and feel compelled to inspect her stockings for runs." He winked and shrugged. "But still, it is what a gentleman does, of course." He waited for her reaction, for her to laugh, smile, nod. But she didn't, and so Kabeer leaned in closer, his face hardening. "OK listen, I know you felt it too, yes? So I am not going to apologize for—"

But she shook her head vigorously, her eyes widening for a moment like she had only just remembered what had happened in the underground garage. "Not that, Kabeer. I mean, well, sure, I can't believe I did *that* either. But it's not what I'm talking about right now."

Kabeer pulled back, frowning. "Then what?"

She turned bright red again, looking down and burrowing her forehead into Kabeer's chest. "Kabeer, all those people we passed on the street . . . and my skirt . . . oh, God, Kabeer, half of Chicago just saw my gigantic thighs and big fat ass!"

And Kabeer just burst out laughing as he pulled Jenny close, hugging her like he had known her for years, perhaps a lifetime. But at the same time it felt so new, so fresh, so . . . different.

"Ah, you were doing the world a favor! A beautiful, healthy woman's body is one of the most wonderful sights imaginable, my dear Jenny! Trust me—every woman out there would have traded places with you in a heartbeat. And any man out there would have traded places with me in a flash. But to hell with them, anyway. Who cares? They are commoners. They are not like us. They are just—"

Jenny pulled away and glanced up at him, eyes narrowed, her mouth open like she was about to snap at him. Kabeer cringed internally at the crude statement—he was too used to moving in circles where people *were* just like him—as he watched Jenny, waiting for her reaction. Would she be angry? Hurt? Insulted?

But Jenny stayed silent. She held that gaze for a moment longer, and then she looked past him and motioned with a head-nod.

"That's the yacht? It's beautiful," she said.

She took a step forward on the wooden jetty, and Kabeer turned and looked at her, not sure what to make of how she brushed off his comment. Who was this woman? She certainly looked interesting. Yes, interesting, unique, and different . . . different from most of the women he ran with.

Kabeer took a breath as Jenny took a step towards the yacht and then stopped, her back to him now. Ya, Allah, those curves, Kabeer thought as that unfulfilled arousal coursed through his body. Natural and full, healthy and . . . and *real*! Ya, Allah, that is what it is, that is what this is, that is what *she* is: Real.

He smiled and shook his head as he took a step towards this somewhat short, supremely contoured, uniquely attractive American woman from who-knows-where. Jenny Jones in her black skirt-suit, no shoes, standing flat-footed in the center of my jetty! That brown hair blown back from the ride through the city. Her soft face flush and peaked from the all the excitement of the last half hour. Oh, shit, she's already under my skin, he thought as he felt his heat spiral higher, leaving no doubt that his need had never gone away, that the ride together, this woman clinging to him, had only pushed him further along.

I must get her alone when we're on this boat, he

thought as he glanced once more at the ways her hips swung as she walked, the way her bottom moved beneath that black skirt, how firm her thighs looked in those tights. Ya Allah, I must get her alone!

It will not be too hard—Father usually takes a nap when we drop anchor far out on the lake. And Yasmeena knows better than to come looking for me when I'm not above decks.

Yes, Kabeer thought as he took one more look at her strong calves, the form in her chest, the curve of her lower back . . . oh, yes, it shouldn't be too hard to get her alone below decks.

And this time, Jenny Jones, I'm not stopping.

With Allah as my witness, I am *not* stopping.

5

Bukhaara III. That was the name of the yacht.

Jenny stared up at the gigantic white boat, its polished hull gleaming in the summer sun. It looked a lot bigger up close, and really, it was way too large to be called a boat. Bukhaara III. Did that mean they had three of these?

She looked down at her shoeless feet, and wiggled her toes inside her tights. Thank God these tights were new. She was still shaking a bit from the sheer courage she had to summon to hike up her skirt and get on the back of that bike, but now that the panic had receded, she could feel a tingling warmth inside her. She thought of how it felt to hold Kabeer tight as he took those turns, the momentum of the ride pushing her body closer to his as the wind roared in her ears. It was the sound of freedom, she thought. It was what she always imagined the sound of freedom would be like.

Freedom, she thought as she looked up at the steel-rimmed gangplank that Kabeer was standing next to, waiting for her to get there. She walked slowly, glancing down at the smooth wood of the jetty as she placed one foot in front of the other, each step giving her a chance to think about what she was doing, to try and sort out what her logic and common sense was telling her from what her body was whispering from somewhere deep inside.

She shook her head and blinked and looked up at that yacht, Sheikh Kabeer Bukhaara standing beside it, waiting for her, his white shirt unbuttoned almost all the way down as he let the sun have at his deeply tanned, brown chest, the ridges of hard muscle casting soft shadows as he smiled unabashedly.

"Faster," he called to her, his grin so wide, so annoyingly perfect, so deceptively . . . genuine?

But Jenny forced herself to take her time walking to the boat, walking towards the Sheikh, walking towards what felt eerily like the beginning of something new, something unexpected, something big.

Well of *course* it's big, Jenny, she told herself as

she diverted her eyes from the Sheikh's steady, un-yielding gaze. I'm finally getting a shot to pitch my idea to someone who can actually finance the invest-ment! And if I get funded, I get to work on what I've dreamed about since little Jenny Jones was baking mud-pies in a make-believe oven! That's what true freedom is, right? The ability to do what you love?

Yes, freedom. That was what she dreamed of when she took her degree, when she set out to chase her dream of starting that restaurant, when she bet ev-erything on it—bet herself on it.

Is that what I'm doing now, she wondered as she smiled at Kabeer as he held out his hand for her to take. Subconsciously putting myself on the negotiat-ing table? The attraction is undeniable, real, impossi-ble to fake. But at the same time I'm not oblivious to the fact that this man is a billionaire, that he seems to be the head of the only investment company that's shown any interest in my proposal, that he basically holds my immediate future in his hands. Just like he had my big round ass cupped in his hands less than an hour ago, she thought as she closed her eyes and shook her head in disbelief.

But the memory of the way he touched her made her tingle, and there was her body butting in and messing up her clear logic, her clean common sense, her focus, her resolve. And now she was at the boat, near the Sheikh, and she grabbed onto Kabeer's outstretched arm as she took the first step onto that gangplank, which suddenly looked very long and rather narrow, almost foreboding, like a warning that she was stepping onto a path that was going to be hard to navigate, a bridge that would take poise and character to cross, a road littered with the broken dreams of women who thought they could juggle the fiery torches of money, sex, and true love without getting burned. Burned to a goddamn crisp.

The gangplank quivered with her weight, and for a moment Jenny wondered if it would give way, sending her plunging into the cool blue waters of Lake Michigan. The suspended stairway swayed as she took another step, but it held firm, and now Kabeer was behind her, his hands lightly positioned on her forearms just beneath her elbows, his pelvis right against her bottom as she held on to the railings and continued to climb.

"About time, Kabeer," came a woman's voice from above. "And what is this? Who is this? Oh, for Allah's sake, Kabeer! This was supposed to be a private meeting. Is this why you were late? I should have known you couldn't—"

Jenny looked up and saw a woman with dark brown hair pulled back tight, sharp features on a long, symmetrical face, and colorless gray eyes that were striking against her dark, Middle-Eastern skin. Those eyes were intense, focused, shamelessly judgmental . . . and they were trained right at her.

"Ah, hello, dear Yasmeena," Kabeer said from behind Jenny.

"Oh!" Jenny said, nervously looking up and blinking. "You're Ms. Yasmeena Bukhaara? Hi! I'm Jennifer Bethany Jones! You sent me an email last week about my business proposal! I was supposed to meet you in your office today! Oh, God, so nice to finally meet you! I'm *so* glad you gave me this opportunity to—"

The woman just stared back like she hadn't heard. No change of expression. "Who? What?" She glanced at Kabeer now, her eyebrows moving a bit. "What is she saying, Kabeer? And can you both *please* walk a bit faster? God! I mean, seriously. Ooof."

That last word sounded like "oaf," and Jenny suddenly felt flustered and even more nervous, and without looking she tried to take the next step, and holy-mother-of-God she straight-up *missed* it! Her foot slid into the space between two steps, and she yelled as a sharp pain ripped through the inside of her thigh as it stretched awkwardly. She grabbed onto both railings as she cried out, but she couldn't stop herself from stumbling, and suddenly panic rolled in as she felt her grip on the left railing loosen, and now she was falling backwards, down, down—

"Got you," Kabeer whispered as he grabbed her, one strong arm snaking around her waist and clamping tight against her stomach, the other grabbing her upper arm firmly, his chest and stomach tightening against her, hips locking tight as his lean, muscular body took on Jenny's entire body weight as he broke her fall.

The gangplank swung wildly as Jenny gasped and flailed, but Kabeer held on, perfectly balanced, like he was in complete control, like he had never lost control, wouldn't lose control, wouldn't let go, wouldn't let her go.

"Shit," she gasped, reaching down and clutching her thigh as she found her balance against the Sheikh's broad, hard body.

"What is it?" he asked. "Did you twist your ankle?"

"No," she said, almost embarrassed. "God, I think I pulled a muscle in my thigh trying to get my balance back."

"Where? Here?" With real concern Kabeer began to reach down the side of her leg, his hand moving down to where her hand was resting on her lower thigh.

"Oh, for—" came Yasmeena's exasperated voice from above, and now she thumped on the gangplank railing and made a clucking noise with her tongue. "All right, Kabeer. I cannot watch this with a straight face. I am instructing the captain to cast off in sixty seconds." She turned away but then turned back for a moment, those disconcerting gray eyes finding their focus on Jenny with alarming accuracy. "That means the gangplank goes up in thirty seconds, whether you two are on it or not."

Jenny tried to look up to see if the woman was

serious, but the catch in her leg was too much for now, and so she just turned wide-eyed to Kabeer as Yasmeena glided out of sight. "She's kidding, right?" Jenny said with a single, nervous chuckle that caught in her throat as she watched three crew members approach the gangplank mechanism above them.

"Yasmeena? Kidding?" Kabeer shook his head. "My sister doesn't do kidding," he said. "OK, come on. We really do need to move. She has done this before. So just hold on, Jenny, all right? I got you."

"What?"

And before she realized what was happening, Kabeer lifted her *clean* off her feet, and she gasped as she threw her arms around his neck as she felt every muscle in his arms and back tense up as he rose to full height. Then he winked at her, and without any sound that betrayed effort, Kabeer literally *carried* her up the gangplank, picking up speed as she held on breathless in his arms, overwhelmed by the exhilarating feeling of him carrying her like she was a feather, a cloud, a wisp of candle smoke.

His strength was surprising, and Jenny's breath caught as Kabeer began to take two steps at a time, his strong legs and lower body propelling the two of them closer to the top, closer, closer, and now with a final leap that made her *bounce* in his arms they were there!

Sure enough, just as Kabeer carefully set her down

on the hard wooden deck, the boat crew cast off the
lines and the gangplank was already off the jetty and
getting pulled in fast before Jenny even had a chance
to straighten her clothes and catch her breath. Kabeer
wasn't joking: His sister didn't do kidding.

Kabeer looked down at her legs and then into her
eyes. "How do you feel? Is there pain? Can you walk?"

Jenny nodded and blinked, her face feeling hot as
her breathing refused to slow down. She suddenly
felt dizzy, faint, like her head was going into a spin,
like her *life* was going into a spin. The unexpected
meeting at the office, that uncharacteristic (for her!)
behavior in the underground garage, that spontaneous (or was it calculated—she didn't know!) act
of kicking off her shoes, hiking her skirt up, racing
through downtown Chicago and along Lakeshore
Drive, clinging to Sheikh Kabeer Bukhaara's hard
body! Then the swinging gangplank, the slip and fall,
the way he caught her, the way he carried her. What
was happening? How can I think straight? I'm on a
billionaire's yacht! My heart is pounding. My head
is spinning. My body is tingling all over. Wait, am I
aroused right now?! Oh, God, I'm seriously going insane! Am I freaking *aroused*?!

And now Jenny just told herself to focus and
f-ing *say something*! "Yes!" she said, the word coming
out embarrassingly loud and squeaky. "I mean no! I
mean, I think so. I mean I can walk. Yeah, sure, I'll
walk. Slowly."

"Come on," Kabeer said, a single bead of sweat rolling down the side of his smooth, flawlessly brown, grinning face. He still wasn't even breathing hard, though. "Let us see if we can find you some shoes to cover up those piggies, yes?"

He grabbed her hand and slowly led her to the accommodations stack, pulling open the door and stepping inside. It was cool and dimly lit, a faint scent of some kind of fragrant oil in the air—dusky but subtle: fresh palm oil perhaps. There was dark brushed wood paneling along the walls, beautifully polished heavy walnut floors, hand-brushed gold-leaf ceilings. Everything about this was rich and elegant, and Jenny felt like she had suddenly stepped into a new world as the door closed behind her, blocking out the sun.

Yes, a new world, she thought as Kabeer led her into a bedroom that looked like what she imagined the Presidential Suite at the Ritz Carlton might look like (she had no idea). He slid open the pinewood floor-to-ceiling doors of a massive closet, revealing a full range of women's clothes on hangers to the left, a shelf unit with perhaps, oh, *forty* pairs of women's shoes to the right! There were at least two pairs of shoes for every occasion one might imagine, including tennis, Jenny was certain. Tennis! On a boat!

"Anything you want," Kabeer said, grinning as he pointed to the closet with a comical flourish, carelessly pulling out a pair of shoes (Jimmy Choo pumps— low end for what was up there . . .) and tossing them to the floor. "Not these, though. These are terrible. Ya, Allah, my sister has terrible taste. Expensive, yes. But terrible." Now he sighed, knocking another pair off the shelf before turning to Jenny. "Here. You pick, I think. I'm sure you have better taste. Or better sense, at least."

"These are your sister's? Ms. Bukhaara's?" Jenny asked, blinking as she remembered the way Yasmeena had looked at her, as if Jenny falling into the lake wouldn't have even fazed the woman. "You know, I'm really not comfortable—"

"Do not be ridiculous. She will not care." Hesitation, then a shrug and that devilish smile that brought out the green in his eyes. "Or rather, she will not notice."

Jenny looked away from the Sheikh and focused on the wall of shoes, and now that dizziness came back, that rush in her head, that tingle in her body. So much going on, suddenly. Had she even eaten today? Oh, God, was she dehydrated? Hypoglycemic? Hyperglycemic? So many shoes. So many *shoes*!

As if he had noticed her hesitation (or perhaps her expression of "what-the-hell-am-I-doing-here-and-god-so-many-shoes" betrayed her incapacity to make a decision about something so strange, minor, and *monumental* . . .), the Sheikh gently touched her arms and carefully pushed her aside, brushing against her body, her hips, her breasts as he stepped in front of her and looked at the closet, his touch lingering for just a moment before he spoke.

"Come on. These are nice. I think they will fit. Here, let me." Kabeer reached up and grabbed a pair of dark red, closed-toe flats that actually looked quite comfortable and would go just fine with her black suit and stockings, so Jenny shrugged as he placed them on the smooth wooden floor by her feet.

"Come," he said, bending down and holding one shoe out. "Come on, Cinderella," he said, looking up at her and winking, his eyes dancing, like he was telling Jenny that if she was Cinderella, then maybe he was the prince who wasn't fooled by the raggedy clothes and the pumpkins.

Jenny placed a hand on his shoulder for support, giggling as she felt him tickle the sole of her foot as she slid into the shoe. But the giggle faded and she inhaled sharply as she felt that muscle in her thigh pull tight as she pointed her toes to get the shoe all the way in.

Kabeer looked up at her, and then down at her leg. He seemed to instantly know she was in pain, and his expression changed and now he motioned to a large cushioned chair not too far away. The smile was gone, the mischief in his eyes replaced by pure authority. "Sit down," he ordered. "Now."

Jenny obeyed, holding onto Kabeer as she limped to the chair. It was dark purple and very soft, and she sank thankfully into it, sighing as she felt it swallow her up.

Kabeer sat on the floor by her feet, taking her left

leg onto his lap. The shoe was off, and Kabeer placed his palm beneath her calf, his other hand reaching just above her knee, where the pain was. Her heel was resting on his upper thigh as he sat cross-legged, and Jenny exhaled now as Kabeer began to rub her aching thigh muscle through her black tights, those same tights he had so crudely "inspected" down in that underground garage—while she had *let* him! It seems so long ago now, doesn't it, Jenny thought as she blinked at the sight of this handsome Sheikh expertly massaging her thigh, his strong fingers kneading and pressing at just the right spot, his stiff thumb burrowing into her soft flesh, finding the tight spot and working it.

"My personal trainer used to work for Tom Brady," Kabeer said. "He showed me how you can literally massage away even a serious muscle injury if you know the right techniques. When Tom had a partially torn calf muscle during practice, this guy got him back on his feet the next day." Kabeer looked up. "That's a six-week injury normally, and my trainer had Tom back at practice like nothing happened."

Jenny nodded, leaning her head back on the cushioned neck-rest. She could feel the pain leaving her as Kabeer massaged her thigh, and she liked how her leg felt so firm and secure in his grip, under his touch, his palm beneath the curve of her calf, her heel gently rocking back and forth on his lap now.

She felt Kabeer shift on the floor, moving closer, and she moved a bit in the chair, pointing her toes forward for a moment. Then she gasped in shock as she felt his hardness move against her soft toes, and when she looked down she blinked when she saw that her foot was resting against the center of Kabeer's trousers, right against his—

Oh, God, she thought as she felt herself move her foot up and down slowly, the feeling of him getting hard beneath her touch arousing her in a way that made it difficult to breathe. She glanced at his face, taking in the way he was looking at her, his gaze narrowed, his breaths becoming short and quick, his heat rising just like his hardness was rising against her foot.

Be careful, a voice inside her whispered. This is not the time to give in to what your body wants, what your flesh needs, what your arousal craves. Your body isn't always right, Jenny, that secret voice rasped. This may feel good . . . *damn* it feels good. But think about what you're doing, where you're taking this.

Think about where this is taking *you*!

I should stop, Jenny thought. But she didn't stop. She told herself she couldn't stop even though deep down she knew that she just didn't want to stop. It had been a hard three years—school, part-time jobs that she hated, all those rejections about her restaurant investment. Her body needed an outlet, didn't it? How long had it been since she had felt this sort of need, this sort of surging desire, raging passion, so sudden, so unexpected, so real. Was it right? Was it proper? Would Grandma approve?

Damn right, she would, Jenny thought in a moment of almost delirious ecstasy, and now she was heating up, her own secret wetness slowly making itself known. Wouldn't Grandma say to just trust your instincts and make the leap, no matter what "society" says is the right thing to do, the proper thing to do, the "womanly" thing to do?

Oh, jump in, Grandma would whisper. Jump in, and trust that the universe will catch you. Jump in, little Jenny! Jump in!

Jenny shivered as she felt goosebumps rise along her arms, those invisible hairs on her neck standing up, that wonderfully warm chill running up and down her legs . . . running between her legs. But this is more than just my body telling me to go on, she thought as she watched herself keep going. It's more than just everyday attraction that's pushing me forward, signaling that it's OK, that it's all right, it's good, it's pure, goddamn *real*.

So Jenny kept going, involuntarily licking her lips now as the Sheikh slowly uncrossed his legs and leaned back on his arms, looking up at her and then down at her foot as she rubbed his hardness firmly now, his girth clearly discernible through the cloth as she got him harder, harder, so *damned* hard.

She couldn't understand what she was doing, why she was doing it, how this man had turned her into some kind of sex-crazed demon in two hours. Again the thought that this man is a billionaire flashed through her mind, and as she smiled at the way his jaw was tightening as he looked at her, she wondered if she truly understood the game she was playing.

Oh, God, am I a whore, she suddenly thought again as Kabeer finally got to his knees, his chest heaving as his hot breath drew near. He was fully hard, the front of his pants strained and peaked in the most captivating way. He's handsome and sexy and God, he turns me on . . . but you can't ignore the fact that his money can set me up with this restaurant, give me the chance to launch my business the way I want, realize my vision for my future. How can I separate those two things? How can I?! Oh, God, what should I do? What should I *do*?!

Kabeer's hands were on her knees now, and he was pushing her legs apart as he drew close. Her skirt was too narrow for her to spread all the way, and now Kabeer stood up and leaned over her, bending down as she looked up at him, looked into his eyes, her mouth opening to receive his kiss.

He bent down and kissed her, with no hesitation, the back of his hand stroking the swell of her breast through her suit jacket. He unbuttoned the single button and opened up her jacket. She exhaled hard as she felt his tongue circle the outside of her lips just as his hands slid beneath her jacket, his fingers teasing forth the outline of her nipple, his thumb and forefinger quickly pinching the sensitive nub to its plump fullness.

"Oh, God, Kabeer," she gasped as he kissed her with fury now, both hands full and firm on her soft breasts, her nipples instantly tightening into raised points as he pinched her hard with those strong fingers, those stiff thumbs.

Now she felt him pull her black fitted blouse up from where it was tucked into her skirt, and she gasped loudly and arched her back as Kabeer pushed the tight stretch cloth up over the globes of her breasts, revealing her black satin bra with the thick underwire. She looked down at herself, mouth open with arousal—God, she looked huge and swollen, she thought, inhaling sharply as Kabeer groaned out loud as he looked down at her milky white cleavage, the way her breasts were pushed up and squished together by that tight bra and the way that soft purple chair was cradling her.

"Oh, God," he whispered, gently running his fingers along the top of each bra cup as she shivered in ecstasy at the way he was teasing her. "Oh, Jenny. You have no idea . . . no *damned* idea how this feels to me, how this looks to me, how badly I want to—"

"Are you *insane!*" came the scream from above and behind them, and Kabeer whipped around as Jenny squealed and tried to push her top back down over her bulging boobs, her shining black bra. "In my room, Kabeer? In *my damn room*?!"

It was Yasmeena, and she made no move to turn her face or even look away while Jenny attempted to get decent. In fact she stared right at Jenny, glancing down at her overflowing boobs with raised eyebrows, hands on her slim hips as she waited for Jenny to pull her jacket back tight over her chest. Only then did Yasmeena blink and look over at her brother, who was sitting back on the floor, looking up at his sister with eyes narrowed, jaw tight, like he was *pissed* at the interruption.

"And are those my shoes?" Yasmeena said, her long arm darting out like an arrow as she pointed at the bright green Jimmy Choo pumps that Kabeer had tossed aside earlier. Now Yasmeena looked over and saw the second pair—the dark red flats that Prince Kabeer had slipped onto Cinderella's feet. The woman's expression hardened, and Jenny could see color rush to her brown face, making her look dark, almost menacing as she towered above the purple sofa that seemed to be pulling Jenny lower and lower, like she was being swallowed by quicksand.

"They fit you well, yes?" Yasmeena said, crossing her arms over her chest now, her white linen shirt crumpling beneath her tight, slender arms. "Fit you as well as that bra fits you, I hope?"

"I . . ." Jenny stammered, feeling the blood rush to her face as she checked to make sure she had gotten that tight top down over her bulging chest.

"She needed shoes, Yasmeena," Kabeer said, not really looking up at his sister. But his tone betrayed his anger. "And I swear I have never seen you wear any of these bloody shoes. So just be calm, yes, sister? We will join you soon." He took a breath and now looked up at his sister. "One more thing, Yasmeena: Regardless of whose room this is, you knew I was in here, and so you damn well *knock* before you walk in here again! Understood?"

Yasmeena took a deep breath, glancing down at her brother and quickly looking up. Jenny really couldn't read her deadpan expression. How old was Yasmeena anyway? Her skin was flawless and tight, not even the finest lines visible around those intense gray eyes. Those eyes though . . . yes, those betrayed a hardness, like she had some years behind her—certainly some experiences behind her, something behind that intensity.

Yasmeena glanced over at Jenny and held her gaze, like she was assessing, evaluating, judging Jenny right there and then, reading what she could in Jenny's big round eyes that were wide like Cinderella's pumpkins right now. Finally Yasmeena blinked, looked up at the ceiling, then at Kabeer, and shook her head in exasperation, reminding Jenny of Kabeer's earlier comment of how Yasmeena thought she was his mother sometimes.

She turned to go, but then, as if in a calculated move, Yasmeena turned her head halfway and said with exceptionally smooth delivery, beautifully calm cadence, perfectly elucidated diction: "I am sorry, respected brother Kabeer. I apologize for not knocking. Now finish up with your whore and—"

But before the words even fully registered with Jenny—and indeed, before Yasmeena even finished uttering her pointed jab—Kabeer *leaped* to his feet, his handsome face suddenly twisted with an anger that shook Jenny, almost scared her, because it seemed to come from a very deep place in this supposedly shallow man.

"By Allah, Yasmeena!" he growled. "You *ever* speak like that again and I swear I will . . . I will . . . I will damned well . . . " The words caught in his throat like he had literally forced them back down, and Kabeer was standing at his full height now, towering over his sister, his forearm flexed, veins rippling in high relief as he pointed his finger at her.

"You will what, little brother?" Yasmeena said, looking up at her "little" brother as he stood a good eighteen inches taller and looked three times broader than the slim Arab woman. "Strike me? Strike your older sister? Is that how a man treats his family? Is that how a leader inspires his followers? Is that how a king rules his people?" She paused now, those gray eyes looking almost silver as they flashed, like Yasmeena had been building to this, like her remark about Jenny was made just to get at Kabeer. "And is that how a Sheikh carries out his God-given duty on this Earth, his duty to his land, his people, his family, his God? Is it, Kabeer?"

Kabeer held the intense eye contact with his older sister for a long time, and Jenny just curled up on that purple chair and tried to disappear into its comfy folds. She watched as Kabeer swallowed once, silently, like Yasmeena's words had found their mark. Now he blinked, and when his eyes opened again after that micro-second of the blink, it was like he had forcibly brought back that devil-may-care billionaire of the tabloids and the gossip pages.

"I do not know, Yasmeena," he said, shrugging like he didn't give a damn. "I do not know how a Sheikh carries out Allah's top secret, mystical commands on this Earth. I do not know because I am not Sheikh. Why don't you ask the Sheikh himself? Father is on board with us, yah?"

Yasmeena stayed expressionless, but Jenny caught just the faintest of movement in her tight, thin lower lip. Was she trying to hold back a *smile*? A smile of some kind of victory over her brother? What the hell kind of family drama have I walked into? Is this just sibling rivalry—something to do with their Sheikdom of Bukhaara—or is it something more complex, something deeper, maybe darker?

Jenny tried not to breath as she could literally taste the tension in the air. Yasmeena had clearly gotten to Kabeer, and after seeing the way the man had used his power of will to force himself to return to his "natural" who-gives-a-shit attitude, Jenny wondered if perhaps there was something deeper to this man, this Arab Sheikh who lived in America and raced around on black motorcycles and frequented the elite bars and nightclubs even though alcohol was not permitted for Muslims.

But now Jenny seemed to remember Cousin Paula saying something about how Kabeer actually never touched alcohol himself when he was out at those clubs and events, in observance of his traditions. So maybe there is something more, Jenny thought as she cast a furtive glance at Kabeer as he stood perfectly still and straight, his jaw still set tight despite the casual persona he had donned. Yes, maybe there is something more to this man. Question is, do I stick around to find out? Or do I turn and walk away now, before anything serious has happened—physical or financial!

Yes, Jenny thought as she glanced at Yasmeena's long brown face, her tight skin, her dark red lips, those gray eyes that flashed so bright against her dark skin. I can't imagine that Yasmeena is going to allow her family's company to invest any money in my idea, to write out a check to a woman she just called her brother's "whore." So what do I have to gain from staying here? More insults? Maybe I say something to Yasmeena that I can't take back? She knows people in the finance world. Maybe I get blacklisted at every potential investment firm in Chicago?! I should cut my losses and get the hell out of here, out of this drama, this dead end, this no-win situation! The boat isn't that far from the dock, right? Can't we pull back and drop me off so I can just take a taxi back to my safe, warm home? My old life? My real life, instead of this alien world of Sheikhs and billionaires and forty pairs of shoes on a boat?

But Jenny wasn't going anywhere, because Yasmeena was standing in the doorway, still staring at her brother, that tight-lipped almost-a-smile expression still on her face. The slight Arab woman in her khaki slacks and white linen shirt looked as formidable as a wall, and so Jenny just took a quick breath so she wouldn't pass out and stayed huddled in that soft purple chair.

Kabeer finally broke the silence. "She is not a whore, Yasmeena. You will apologize to her," he said quietly, carefully, calmly but with an underlying seriousness that affected Jenny in the strangest of ways. It was like he actually gave a shit about how Yasmeena spoke about her. Yes, Kabeer's reaction wasn't just to get to

Yasmeena. It was real, genuine, a protective instinct that seemed so old-fashioned in a way.

Yasmeena glanced at Jenny again, rolled her eyes, and then shook her head and turned. "I am sorry," she said as she walked out the door, speaking without turning her head before moving to the stairs. "I forgot. Kabeer is the whore in this family."

Kabeer laughed as he walked to the door and slammed it shut. He shook his head as he walked back to Jenny. "Too serious! She needs some romance in her life, I think," he said with a wink.

Jenny raised her eyebrows and smiled politely, not sure what to do next. But for some reason she felt calm, like somehow she knew Kabeer a lot better now, even though technically she didn't know jack about the guy. "You should probably head upstairs," she said quietly. "I'll stay here." Then a quick smile, spontaneous and sweet. "Maybe in a different room though, yeah?"

Kabeer snorted. "You are heading above decks with me, Jenny. Come on. I will help you."

Jenny blinked three times as she thought about that jetty and that taxi ride home. But the panic passed quick and the words kept coming, almost too easy. "My thigh feels fine," she said brightly. "Besides, I thought you had a private family meeting."

"It is a business meeting. All our family meetings are business meetings. There is nothing else in my family. At any rate, you must join this meeting because you are now on the agenda."

Jenny looked up. "What?"

Kabeer shrugged. "You came to Bukhara Capital to pitch a business plan, yes? So pitch it! My father and sister are upstairs, and together we are the entire executive committee of our firm. And you have most certainly got everyone's attention now."

Jenny swallowed hard as the thought of pitching her idea to Yasmeena and the older Sheikh of Bukhaara made her stomach seize up tight like a fist. Was she getting seasick, she wondered. Or is this just your standard, everyday, straight-up *panic*?!

"Are you ready?" Kabeer asked now, a slow, deliberate smile breaking on his face, like he was challenging her, daring her, asking her to show him what she was made of. "Are you ready, Jenny Jones?"

Jenny swallowed again, blinking as she got a distinct feeling that she was at a crossroads here, where her next choice would have dramatic consequences on her life. The feeling was strange, eerie, almost otherworldly, and for some reason it took all the panic away. Now she was breathing normally, and as she stood, wincing a bit as her thigh muscle strained but then held up, she straightened her skirt and buttoned her jacket. She looked down at Yasmeena's shoes, and took a long, careful breath. Then she stepped into those shoes like she was stepping into her own future, taking in a deep breath as she felt Kabeer silently reach out and offer his sturdy arm for support.

Now Jenny Jones, food-lover and aspiring chef, part-time MBA from City College of Chicago, future head-chef and restaurant proprietor, stood up to her full height of around five-foot-and-very-little, and looked at Kabeer Bukhara, billionaire Arab Sheikh, man who had kissed her lips, touched her body, turned her on in the most unexpected, perhaps unwanted, certainly untimely way . . . yes, she looked confidently into his dark green eyes and, doing her best not to blink, said:

"Damn right I'm ready. I've been ready for this meeting for a long, long time. So bring it."

6

"**G**lobal Kitchen, right?"

Jenny squinted in the sun, carefully sitting on the white canvas chair across from Yasmeena. Kabeer hadn't even officially introduced her to Yasmeena, or to the older, distinguished-looking man with a thick, long white beard that perfectly matched his immaculately white flowing robe that was tradition-al Arab dress.

The man sat in a deck chair that was reclined, and his eyes were closed tight. His lips were moving, and for a moment Jenny thought he was praying under his breath; but then she saw the earpiece tucked in his right ear and the lit-up phone on the round glass table that was fixed to the deck beside the chair. The older Sheikh Bukhaara was quietly talking in Arabic, his voice low but the words still coming across in fragments to Jenny. The language sounded nice, Jenny thought as she listened to the older man's relaxed delivery. Mysterious, foreign, harsh at times but still beautiful.

Yasmeena was seated on a straight-backed wooden chair. She had sunglasses on now, but with a very light tint and Jenny could clearly see her eyes. God, they looked that silvery-gray even through sunglasses! Still, there was a different air about the woman now. Perhaps it was because she was with her father? Or maybe Jenny just felt that way because Yasmeena had asked her that question, the question that made Jenny's heart jump as the adrenaline flowed, reminding her that this was her shot. However twisted the path to this point, she was now pitching her idea, and clearly Yasmeena had read her proposal.

"Global Kitchen, right?" Yasmeena had asked as Jenny made her way up the metal stairs to the top deck of the boat, holding tight to both handrails as she favored that thigh which was actually feeling fine now—maybe Kabeer was serious about massaging away the injury.

Jenny nodded now, still squinting a bit. "Yes," she said. "Global Kitchen. I thought the name captures the—"

"I hate it," Yasmeena said.

"What?"

"The name. I hate it. It sounds like a . . . like a food court at one of your local shopping malls!"

"OK . . ." Jenny felt her life—or at least her carefully-rehearsed presentation—flash before her eyes. She hates the name?! That was the *last* thing I expected to have to defend!

She blinked as she tried to recalibrate, tried to figure out if she should argue for the name right now or try to steer the conversation to something more substantive. The sun felt very harsh suddenly, the way it reflected off the blue waters of Lake Michigan. The yacht had cast off not so long ago, but the towers of downtown Chicago looked alarmingly small already as the yacht plowed through the waves, heading for Canada, it seemed. The wind blew through her dark brown hair, whipping it back and around as Jenny struggled to tame it back into a messy ponytail as she looked at Yasmeena and then at Kabeer, who was listening but was uncharacteristically quiet.

Now the older man was off the phone and he calmly, gracefully looked over to the group, glancing briefly at Jenny without acknowledging her, and then looking over at Yasmeena.

What, am I invisible? Jenny thought. Do these people even notice other human beings?

"Did you tell her our opinion about the name?" Sheikh Bukhaara said in a resonant, deep voice that nonetheless seemed to take the man some effort to make it heard through the wind and the roar of the engines.

Yasmeena nodded, making eye contact with her father and then looking down and staying silent. The man turned to Jenny now. "We do not like the name," he said. "Global Kitchen sounds like a . . . like a cheap restaurant at the Cincinnati Airport."

From the corner of her eye Jenny saw Kabeer smile and turn away, as if he was stifling a laugh. What's the joke, she wanted to ask him. Am I the joke here, she suddenly thought. Did you bring me up here for your family's amusement? Should I stand up and perform some tricks for you and your royal family now?

But Jenny held her calm and looked firmly at Sheikh Bukhaara. "I'm open to suggestions on the name," she said, doing her best to match Sheikh Bukhaara's tone (and doing a pretty good job of it, if she did say so herself . . .) "But the name is secondary. What's important is the idea, the vision. Let's talk about that first. You've obviously seen the proposal and business plan. If not, I've got a copy—"

Sheikh Bukhaara waved his arms and leaned back in his reclining deck chair. The wind played with his long white beard as he grunted and then gestured towards Yasmeena, his gaze still trained on Jenny. "I do not care about the details of the idea. Yasmeena has analyzed it and briefed me on it. She likes it and I trust her judgment. You like it, yes, Yasmeena?"

Yasmeena nodded again, slowly but clearly, and

now Jenny looked at her in surprise. "Really?" she said, an involuntary smile breaking on her smooth round face.

Yasmeena gave her father a quick look before glancing back at Jenny. "But of course the restaurant business is notoriously hard," she said. "Especially at the high-end level where you want to play." She sighed now, like she was reluctant to say what was coming next. "But your plans for expanding this into a franchise that could go national, even international . . . well, that is something . . . something unique. Well thought out. It is a strong and clear vision, which I do not often see in first-time entrepreneurs. Yes, it is something that could do well if it's done right."

"It could be very big, you told me," Sheikh Bukhaara said in that deep voice, and now when Jenny looked at the old man she swore she saw a hint of mischief in his tired eyes, like he was teasing his straight-laced, overly-serious daughter, trying to playfully embarrass her. "What was it you said, Yasmeena? It was an American expression. Ah, yes: Big time! You said it could be *big time*, right, Yasmeena?" He spread his arms out wide now, and with his white robes billowing in the wind and that beard looking wild as the wind whipped it all over, the man looked like some kind of mystical sage, a magical druid.

"You said 'big time,' Yasmeena? Where did you learn that expression?" Kabeer asked now, his tone more taunting than teasing, but still reasonably playful—

at least compared to the interchange that had just occurred below decks. "What American TV have you been watching, dear sister?"

Yasmeena seemed unmoved, and if she was embarrassed or even amused, Jenny couldn't tell. "Like I said, the restaurant business is very tough. It will be nothing if it is not done right. If it is done right, it could do well."

Jenny took a deep breath as she tried to control her excitement. "Just have to make sure it's done right," she said with the enthusiasm of a girl scout about to tie her first knot or bake her first cookie.

The old man clapped his hands and raised them to the sky as if he was saying "God willing" or something. Kabeer laughed out loud behind her, and it was a supportive, admiring laugh that made Jenny feel warm all over. Even Yasmeena's expression looked less severe for a moment as Jenny's excitement spread through the group, and for a moment Jenny got a strange feeling like she was a part of something, a part of this, a part of . . . a part of this family.

But Yasmeena was still all business. "Easier said than done. Everything will depend on getting the first location off to a flying start. If the first restaurant fails—or even does just average—there will be no hope for expansion. The first restaurant has to be big. Heavy publicity. Influential reviews. And, of course, a celebrity chef."

"Celebrity chef," Jenny said, nodding and taking a

deep breath. "I know that the traditional model for a successful high-end restaurant is to have a famous chef as head of the kitchen. But like I said in my proposal, I would actually be the head chef. That's part of *my* model. I've been cooking my whole life, and I've been experimenting with all kinds of exotic foods, innovative combinations, exciting mixes of international cuisines! My proposal includes a full section on menu options and layouts, and—"

"I read the section on the food, Ms. Jones," Yasmeena said dismissively. "The concept is good and the menu looks fine for now. And in fact you can still be in charge of the menu and request that the head chef include your ideas. But you cannot *be* the head chef. You have no qualifications, no experience, no reputation, no—"

"I have the *skills*," Jenny snapped. "That's what matters, isn't it? In the end a restaurant is about how the food tastes, right?"

Yasmeena shrugged as if she couldn't care less. "Yes, I suppose a restaurant is about the food. But it is not *all* about the food. Every day in the world new restaurants are opening—new restaurants that serve excellent food. And you know something: eighty percent of those restaurants will be out of business before Ramadan."

"Ramadan? Well, isn't that the fasting season anyway?" Jenny said, and she wanted to dive off that deck as she heard herself say it. "Ohmygod, I'm so sorry! I didn't mean it like that! It was just—"

Yasmeena raised her eyebrows and glanced over at her father, but the old man had his eyes closed now, and this time it looked like he wasn't on the phone and had actually dozed off. Kabeer had stepped away from the group, and Jenny could see him on the phone at the far end of the long, windy deck. He had dark wayfarers on, and he was smiling and laughing as he spoke, his body language looking almost flirtatious, Jenny thought for a moment.

And now that earlier warm feeling of being part of the family seemed lost and unregainable, and Jenny felt like everything was suddenly turning dark and menacing, and she had made a culturally insensitive joke, and Yasmeena was going to have her thrown overboard, and Kabeer was teasing and flirting on the phone with someone, and . . . and . . and focus, you moron. *Focus*!

Calmness again. Control once more. Breathing normal. You can handle this, Jenny told herself. You can handle *anything*!

And as if the universe was still watching, still listening, still testing her, that wild wind died down and the blazing sun went behind a cloud for a moment and Yasmeena miraculously seemed unfazed by the quip about Ramadan.

"Yes, Ramadan is the month of fasting for all Muslims," she said matter-of-factly. "But it is not like people do not eat for a month. The fasting period is from sunrise to sunset, so at night there are great feasts in all Muslim countries!" Now those gray eyes lit up, and even through those sunglasses Jenny could see some emotion come through. "Oh, the midnight feasts in Bukhaara! Kabeer and I would run through the streets, followed by the horse-drawn carriages with Father and our mothers and the royal attendants. We would eat freshly picked dates offered by the street-vendors. Fragrant rice pilafs, the purest white grains perfectly fluffy and plump, infused with saffron, decorated with streaks of orange and green food coloring!"

Jenny smiled as she pictured the scene: the Middle-Eastern city of Bukhaara lit up at midnight, the narrow streets crowded with joyful, colorfully dressed people feasting on fresh dates, sweet rice, savory kebabs. The domes and minarets lit up in the night, the rolling sand dunes looking silver beneath the starlit desert skies.

The image was so strong in her mind that Jenny felt that otherworldly, eerie sense once more, that sense that had pushed her to keep going . . . keep chasing her dream, keep following her instincts . . . her instincts with this business, her instincts with . . . Kabeer?

But this was time to talk business, and Jenny knew

it. So she nodded and smiled at Yasmeena and told herself to keep going.

"That sounds wonderful," she said, meaning every word. "I can almost picture you and Kabeer as children. Is it just the two of you, or are there more—"

"We had an older brother. He is no more," Yasmeena said, and she spoke quickly, abruptly, without emotion, and Jenny immediately wished she hadn't asked the damn question!

Stick to the topic, moron, she told herself as she cringed at her last two missteps. Talk food. Talk the restaurant. Close the deal. Don't ask personal questions! These aren't your friends! This isn't your family!

"I'm sorry to hear that," Jenny said, and before she could stop herself, she was stumbling forward. "I'm sorry to bring it up."

Yasmeena ignored the apology, but whatever emotion she had shown was now buried again. "Like I was saying, food is just one part of what makes a restaurant successful. I know you'd *like* it to be all about the food. Every restaurant owner—and certainly every chef—wants it to be all about the food. But it is *never* all about the food, and, quite honestly, Ms. Jones, I assumed you would have already understood that as a businesswoman."

Jenny seethed at being talked to like a child, but she knew Yasmeena was right. Great food and a creative menu was necessary but not sufficient for success. Not in a high-stakes, competitive market like the high-end restaurant business, where you need to invest a lot of money up front and just a couple of bad months can sink you. You can't take the chance that the food alone will get you there. Marketing, perception, press, *buzz* . . . that's what gets the tables booked, that's what gets people to tell their friends, that's what puts a restaurant over the top. That's what gets you to the big time.

So Jenny nodded as she held eye contact with Yasmeena. Then she shrugged and looked away for a moment. "OK," she said quietly, realizing quickly that the easiest and best way to build buzz was indeed to hire a celebrity chef. "So we hire a celebrity chef. Maybe poach one from another restaurant?"

Yasmeena shook her head like she had already thought about it. "That will not work. The big names are going to want to bring in their own menus, their own vision. The restaurant would become *their* restaurant, and that would take away from your story."

"My story?" Jenny said, frowning, her face scrunching up in the way that Grandma always got after her about.

"Your story. Americans love the underdog story, yes? You know: lower class girl works her way through a part-time MBA, starts a unique restaurant that sources local food and serves creative dishes that draw from the world's cuisines. It is a good story. It will play well both here and abroad, once you expand overseas. Your lower-class background and non-flashy education will fight the perception of white Americans being privileged and entitled."

Lower-class girl? If they weren't on a boat, Jenny would have stood and walked right out of there. My parents may not have been around a lot, but that's because they worked *hard*, little Miss Silver-Spoon-up-the-Butt! We lived in a warm, clean *house*, not a goddamn trailer park with meth-addicts for neighbors. I am not trailer-trash, you stuck-up—

But wait, Jenny thought as she pulled her emotions back into line. The truth was, she'd thought of that angle herself, thought of that story herself. And in a way it was true, wasn't it? Money *had* been tight growing up. They hadn't always lived in a safe neighborhood when she was little. Both her parents worked long hours and weren't often the nicest, most understanding parents when it came down to it. Jenny had worked her way through community college. Her degree had been in accounting, even though she would have loved to have gone to culinary school. Accounting had gotten her a part-time job in the finance department for the McDonald's Corporation, and she had learned a lot about how franchises and expansion was handled. That job had only lasted a year or so before she was downsized and had to work three other jobs, but it helped give her the confidence that she could handle the finances of her own restaurant chain when it came down to it.

So yes, it was a good story, Jenny realized. *She* was a good story. And Yasmeena was right again—a really big celebrity chef would overshadow Jenny's story, stifle her vision. She wouldn't be able to train a true celebrity chef, teach them her own creations. The ego battles would be too much.

Now Jenny looked at Yasmeena with a modicum of respect. This woman knew her business. She was legit. And what's more, from the way she was talking, it sounded like she had already decided to fund Jenny's venture.

The realization hit home just as Jenny had the thought, and her heart almost stopped as she tried to come to terms with the fact that she was sitting on a yacht, the skyline of Chicago in the distant background, the rich blue waters of Lake Michigan all around . . . yes, she was sitting on a yacht with the owners of Bukhaara Private Capital, discussing how to make her restaurant—her vision, her creation, her *dream*—come true!

Her heart pounded as she listened to Yasmeena talk about the proposal. The woman had clearly read it in detail, and so it was odd that she seemed surprised when Jenny had introduced herself earlier, while walking up the gangplank. Maybe she didn't hear her? Whatever. That didn't matter. What mattered was that Yasmeena seemed to be running the show at Bukhaara Capital, and she was clearly interested in Jenny's idea.

Yasmeena had been talking, but a lot of it was flowing right through Jenny as she felt waves of elated disbelief rock her body as she sat there in her business suit. This was a yes! They were going to fund it! Weren't they? Aren't you? Oh, God, don't tell me you were leading me on just to crush me at the last minute! Oh, Yasmeena, you cruel, evil—

"So yes," Yasmeena said, nodding and looking right at Jenny. "I'm going to recommend that we provide the seed money for starting your venture, Ms. Jones. Assuming we are in agreement about bringing in the right celebrity chef." She stood up now, straightening her delicately creased khaki pants. "You'll have our offer sheet by tomorrow."

Jenny swallowed. What's happening, she asked herself. Is this the offer? Is this really it? Oh, my God, is this it? This is it, isn't it! She almost burst into a combination of tears and hysterical laughter—she'd imagined this moment for so long, and now it was here, in the most unexpected way possible, from the most unexpected person possible!

But even though she was dancing inside, she held her poker face (somewhat) and nodded like the experienced businesswoman she wanted to be, and she said, "Thank you, Yasmeena. I look forward to reviewing the terms of your offer. Can I get back to you in a week, once I receive the term sheet?"

Yasmeena snorted. "Ms. Jones," she said cordially. "You will be offered our standard, boilerplate term sheet. The numbers are non-negotiable and final. So unless you have another offer from a competing investment firm of our caliber, you'll get back to me before this boat docks at Navy Pier. Are we clear? You have about forty-five minutes."

Jenny sat stunned as a seagull screeched from the flagpole to her left. She had no other offer, and although she thought about bluffing just so she could hold her own and not look like a pushover, she knew she had her back against the wall.

"I'll let you know before we dock," Jenny said in a voice that was barely more than a whisper. "Thank you, Yasmeena."

Yasmeena turned towards the front of the boat, facing into the wind, which plastered her clothes against her body. She looks frail and malnourished, Jenny thought. How is it that a woman whose best memories from childhood revolve around food seems to have lost the gift for enjoying that part of life?

"Good," Yasmeena said, speaking over her shoulder without even looking at Jenny. "Oh, and don't call me Yasmeena, Ms. Jones. We're not friends."

"Yes . . . Ms. Bukhaara," Jenny said after a long pause, during which she forced down a big slice of the Bukhaara-recipe humble pie. "Of course."

Now old Sheikh Bukhaara emerged from where he had been dozing off in his chair. He stretched his arms and looked around, as if he wasn't sure where he was. "All right," he announced. "I am going to retire below decks to continue this excellent nap. Very good job, Yasmeena. I'm proud of you, child."

Yasmeena turned and smiled—perhaps the first real smile Jenny had seen on the woman. The old Sheikh placed a hand on her shoulder as he walked by, and Yasmeena almost glowed for a moment.

Kabeer sauntered up to the group now, still holding his phone like he was expecting a call or message. He looked lost in thought, and Jenny looked up at him, wondering if it was right that she felt a bit miffed at him walking off, leaving her to pitch her idea one-on-one with Yasmeena.

No, it isn't right, she told herself. Grow up. Don't misinterpret the attraction you feel for him, the attraction that he seems to feel for you. It's probably nothing more than dumb animal lust, and to think it means something more is childish, immature, and, well, pretty dumb. And you're not dumb, Jenny. You might be slightly in over your head, slightly rumpled and turned around by the madness of today, but you aren't dumb. So stop expecting Kabeer to suddenly behave like he's got your back, like he's going to take care of you. Stop thinking that you can trust him.

The old Sheikh walked past Kabeer, glancing up at his son. Jenny saw none of the pride and warmth that Yasmeena had received, and in fact it was almost a cold, accusing look that the older Sheikh Bukhaara shot as a silent attendant dressed in sailor whites helped the man to the stairwell.

"Yes, good job, Yasmeena," Kabeer said, clapping three times as he walked towards his sister. "I caught the bit about the celebrity chef, and I think it is a wonderful idea. In fact, here is another wonderful idea. Come, let us talk for a moment."

Kabeer and Yasmeena walked towards the front of the gleaming upper deck and began speaking in Arabic. Jenny watched and listened, once again enjoying the strange, exotic sounds of the foreign language as Kabeer spoke with some excitement, even passion, to his older sister. She barely moved as he spoke, but then suddenly she almost doubled over with an incredulous laugh that sounded not unlike those screeching seagulls.

"Absolutely not, Kabeer," she said in English, her voice coming through as the wind suddenly changed direction, carrying the sound back to Jenny, and for a moment Jenny wondered if Yasmeena *wanted* her to hear this part. "I warned you after the Holbrook deal," Yasmeena continued, her voice sharp and clear. "You do *not* get to use Bukhaara Capital as your playground for whatever new, fun experience you're seeking! You have to learn how to separate your business and personal life. You see how I do it—you think I *wanted* to make the offer to this tramp you brought on board? But I read her proposal a month ago and the business plan is solid. It could be big, and my responsibility is to choose businesses that could be big, even if I do not like the people involved. You can do whatever the hell you want with this woman—and Allah knows you will do what you want with her—but you are *not* involved with this deal."

"Then there is no deal," Kabeer said, his look calm and unwavering as he stared his sister down. "I am an equal partner in Bukhaara Capital, and you know that both of us need to approve any new investment. I get what I want, or there is no deal."

Yasmeena took off her sunglasses. "All right, Kabeer," she said, glancing over at Jenny and then back at her brother like she smelled victory. "No deal." She snorted pointedly at Kabeer. "Now do you think she will let you near those monstrous breasts again?"

Um, I can hear you, Jenny wanted to say, but she held back and listened in disbelief.

Kabeer flinched and glanced over at Jenny to see if she had heard. He held her gaze for less than a second, but there was something in his look that told her to stay calm, to not lose her cool, to . . . to trust him.

"I do not give a damn whether she lets me touch her again or not," Kabeer said. "I have swimsuit models and beauty queens calling me ten times a goddamn day. You are a fool if you think I am doing this to be close to this woman I barely know." Now he turned and faced his sister directly, hands on his tight hips, his broad chest straining the few buttons that were still fastened on his fitted white dress shirt. "But it does not matter, because I know you are bluffing. The reason you can separate your business life and your personal life is because you *have* no damned personal life. It is all business, Yasmeena! And I know you want this deal."

Yasmeena was silent, but Jenny saw her blink hard, saw her flinch in that wind-blown top.

But Kabeer wasn't done. He was aggressive and firm, and he was going in for the kill, in a way closing the deal on his terms. "But the biggest thing is that you *know* my idea makes sense, has merit, is innovative and unusual and will get attention. And all publicity is good publicity, yes? So I am correct. I know it and you know it." He tilted his head back and laughed—not in a mocking way, but in an innocent, almost schoolboyish manner, perhaps in the same way he had laughed with his sister while affectionately teasing her as a child back in their Sheikdom of Bukhaara. "I am calling your bluff, Yasmeena. It is my way or no way. I am not backing down. You know I will not back down."

Yasmeena was silent for a very long, tense moment, and then she put her sunglasses back on and walked over to where Jenny was sitting with arms crossed over her "monstrous" boobs and a twisted frown on her normally sweet face.

"I know how to separate my personal feelings from a business relationship," Yasmeena said tersely as she walked past Jenny. "And if you want to see this restaurant of yours succeed, I hope you figure out how to do the same, Ms. Jones. Congratulations and good luck. You've made your soup, and now I hope you like the taste."

And just like that Yasmeena was gone, like she was a vampire who could turn into a seagull, and suddenly it was just Jenny and Kabeer. Jenny looked over at the grinning Sheikh-Prince-billionaire-whatever as he walked towards her, one deliberate step after another, the wind outlining his muscular, ripped body as it pressed his fitted clothes flat against his ridged torso, magnificently muscled stomach and hips, powerful thighs . . .

"Kabeer, what the hell is—" she said, but then stopped.

Because Kabeer was very close to her now, and with that couldn't-give-a-shit grin still on his face, he stretched his arms out wide and looked down at himself like a TV game-show host presenting himself, like he was the impressive prize being shown, the jackpot, the star of the show.

And with those green eyes shining bright like two emeralds in the desert sun, Sheikh Kabeer Bukhaara smiled wide and proclaimed to all that could hear, "Jenny Jones: Meet your new celebrity chef."

7

"**N**ow?" Kabeer said to the dark attendant in the white clothes who stood at the top of the steps, at the far end of the upper deck. "Father wants to see me now? I thought he was asleep."

"The Sheikh has asked for you," the attendant said, bowing his head and simply repeating the sentence he had uttered a moment ago, when he nervously stepped onto the deck and plucked up the courage to interrupt Kabeer and Jenny.

Kabeer glanced over at Jenny, and it occurred to him that perhaps it would actually be a good thing if this woman had some time to herself right now. She looked shellshocked at his announcement—indeed, Kabeer himself was not sure what he had been think- ing when he insisted on being the head chef! Still, it was clearly a bigger shock for her, one of perhaps many unexpected, shocking things he had thrown at her today. No doubt Kabeer was impressed at how she had handled the events of the day thus far without losing her composure, without breaking down into tears like he had seen many others do under Yasmee- na's gaze. Still, perhaps it was best if she had a few minutes of space—just like he had given her some space by backing off during the meeting.

Yes, he had been watching and listening as Jenny dealt with his shark of a sister—indeed, in a spon- taneous, almost perverse move Kabeer had decided to fake a phone call so he'd have an excuse to step back and watch this sweet, innocent, curvy Ameri- can woman stumble and crumble, fall and flail, get chewed up and spat out by Yasmeena.

So Kabeer had stepped away and talked loudly to a silent phone as he paid close attention to how this curious woman Jenny navigated her way through that conversation with Yasmeena. And, by Allah, the American woman won! She may not know it, but to get Yasmeena to offer her a term sheet after just one meeting?! It was a victory!

That puzzled Kabeer in a way too. Yes, certainly Jenny's idea was good—perhaps even great. But Yas-

meena turned down great ideas every day! His sister
knew that launching a new business was much more
about the person than the idea or concept, and so if
Yasmeena had agreed to put Bukhaara Capital's money into Jenny's business, it really meant that Yasmeena, in her own way, was expressing confidence
in Jenny herself! Jenny's character. Her intelligence.
Her capacity to follow through.

Ya Allah, Kabeer thought as he dismissed the
now-shaking attendant and then glanced at Jenny,
who had turned away from him and now stood against
the railing looking directly into the endless blue of
the vast great lake, away from the distant skyline of
Chicago. Kabeer took a long breath as he glanced at
her full, womanly figure from behind. Her clothes
were pressed tight against her body, highlighting her
curves in a way that made him sweat more than the
damn sun ever could. The summer wind swept her
brown hair back like a flag in a hurricane, open and
free, the wildness contrasting with her professional
skirt suit in a way that made Kabeer yearn to figure
out the mystery of this woman, this woman who pos-
sessed a strangely attractive mix of self-consciousness
and confidence, insecurity and a deep sense of self-
worth, vulnerability and . . . and . . . power!

Mother of God, this woman had in some way ex-
erted power over both him and his sister today, had
she not? Had she not stopped Kabeer in the parking

lot when she herself was aroused? Had she not some-how set aside the anger and indignation she must have felt when Yasmeena called her a whore in that first meeting? Yes, set aside the anger well enough to have a business conversation and get the deal she came to get!

And now Kabeer wondered if Jenny would have stopped him downstairs in Yasmeena's room too. Would she have let him get close and then backed away, reminding him that this was a business meet-ing first, that she was here to make her pitch, sell her idea, close her deal? Did this woman have that in her? Was she playing that game? Perhaps playing it without even realizing it?

Kabeer looked at Jenny again, his mind turning as he blinked hard into the wind. Is this woman capable of playing that game, he wondered as his breathing quickened and then slowed. That old, ancient game that mixed power and money, love and sex, influence and desire . . .

Kabeer was no stranger to women who tried to play that game—some were good at it, some not so good, and some not sure if they wanted to play it but did not have the strength of character to stay true to themselves when exposed to Kabeer's power and influence, his potent mixture of charm and . . . and, well, money. Of course, Kabeer understood that any relationship, no matter how deep or shallow, is a game, a dance between two people, a stage production sometimes.

But there is nothing about this woman that is an act, is there, he thought now as he remembered that his father was waiting and he could not linger here and think himself into circles trying to figure out the riddle of this American woman who he barely knew and who was already under his skin in the most unexpected of ways.

Yet Kabeer stood there, taking in the sight of her standing against that railing, her dark, wild hair looking striking against the blue of the surf and sky. She stood with her back straight, her shapely legs braced slightly apart as she held on to that railing and looked out over the horizon.

What are you looking at, Jenny Jones? What do you see out there? Do you see your future? Yes, little Jenny with your big brown eyes, round and innocent but with a fire that sets ME afire!

Do you see your future, dear Jenny? Am I in it, Kabeer wanted to whisper in her ear as he slipped his arms around her waist, grasping her tight, pushing her against that railing as she backed up against his body.

Am I in it, and does it feel like this, he would whisper as he kissed her soft neck, her smooth cheeks, her full lips, his arms tightening their hold on her, his body hardening as he moved closer, pinning her against the metal railing as the wind screamed in their ears.

Will she resist me, he wondered as he took a step closer, his breathing quickening as his thoughts suddenly evaporated, leaving nothing but pure, savage, unfulfilled *need*. Will she shout for me to stop as I hold her tight against that strong metal railing and *ravish* her the way my body wants, the way my body needs, the way my body goddamn *craves* right now, has craved since I first touched her haunting curves down in that dark basement garage? Will she scream when I hold her thick brown hair tight, pull her head back, kiss her the way I yearn to kiss her? Will she struggle when I undress her, quickly, ripping off buttons, tearing through cloth, right here, right now, on this open deck, under the wild blue sky, beneath the all-seeing eyes of Allah?

Another step closer, and now the blood was pounding in his ears and the sun felt blinding as he approached her from behind. He could smell her faint perfume, her unique musk . . . oh, God, he wanted this woman, wanted to touch her again, take in her smell, her taste . . . he wanted to damn well *consume* her if he could!

Ya, Allah! Kabeer almost shouted out loud as he abruptly turned and stormed down the metal stairs, and suddenly he was in the cool, quiet, air-conditioned atmosphere of the walnut-paneled interior hallways of this million-dollar yacht, the wind and sunlight gone, leaving him almost disoriented as he stood and caught his breath, regained his frame, his goddamn sanity.

Slowly Kabeer began to walk towards his father's cabins at the far end of the yacht, and only now, as he forced his arousal for Jenny to take a backseat because he needed to think clearly for a moment . . . yes, only now did he realize that he had made a profound mistake with this whole chef business.

I am not going to be able to keep my hands off this woman, he thought as he walked down the empty, silent hallway that smelled of sandalwood incense and palm oil. I know myself. I know what my body feels, what my body needs, what my body damn well craves. And right now it is her, Jenny Jones, whether I like it or not. So now I have thrown myself into this chef business, which means I am committing to working with her—working with her closely, every day for months, a year, maybe more! If I take this woman the way I want to take her—and I damned well am *going* to take her—then what happens a few months from now, a year from now, two years from now? I am part of her business—and not just her business: now that Bukhaara Capital is investing, it becomes Bukhaara's business as well. Part of the family business, yes?! Yasmeena will be watching. Father will be watching. God will be watching. Ya, Allah, what have I stepped into here? What was I thinking?!

Kabeer knew that if he started down the path of

being the head chef to launch Jenny's restaurant with some buzz, he would need to follow through. He would actually need to be *good* at his work. He would actually need to *show up* at work.

Of course, Kabeer knew he was capable of following through once he had a goal in mind—indeed, he had achieved excellence in all sorts of physical and intellectual fields: squash champion at Paris-Sorbonne, law review at Columbia. There had been martial arts belts, solo skydiving certifications, competition-level equestrian riding. Yes, Kabeer had the patience and dedication to achieve a goal once the goal was set. But what was the goal here?

Yes, Kabeer, he asked himself as the thick wooden door to the old Sheikh's room appeared at the end of the long, wood-paneled hallway. What is the bloody goal here? Is it just the experience? The fun of it? The thrill of something new?

Or perhaps the thrill of something old . . .

And now Kabeer was swept back to those lingering memories of childhood, of happy days in old Bukhaara, when the royal family was truly a family. Sheikh Bukhaara's two wives—Yasmeena's mother and his own mother—in the large open kitchen in the eastern chambers of the palace. The two queens considered it their sacred duty to supervise the preparation of the family meals, and the mornings were always the happiest times of young Kabeer's days as the royal children played in the sprawling chambers as they watched their mothers, the queens, the Sheikhas of Bukhaara, chattering away with each other, calling out instructions to the veiled attendants who bustled around the kitchen, chopping and cutting, mixing and rolling, grinding fragrant spices, tenderizing fresh meat, baking Arabian flatbreads while that pure, saffron-flavored rice bubbled to completion in the background.

Of course, in the happiest of days it was three royal children who played in those vast, lavish chambers, laughing and yelping as they bounced on the silk-covered daybeds, clambered over the ancient teak-wood tables that sat low to the ground, splashed through the shallow fountains lined with the finest Italian marble and studded with diamonds that flashed like stars under a new moon, emeralds green as wet summer grass, rubies red like . . . red like . . . red . . .

Stop it! Kabeer told himself as he prepared to enter the Sheikh's chambers. For a moment he felt sick as the yacht lurched over a swell in the waters, and he almost turned away. But Kabeer didn't get seasick. The sickness was not in his body but in his mind.

Stop thinking about it, he told himself again as he touched the cool wooden door to his father's chambers. But now Kabeer was that child again suddenly, standing outside his father's private chambers in the Royal Palace, shivering in his little princely robes as he waited to be summoned. The memory of that feeling—that feeling of despair, fear, *guilt*—was so strong that Kabeer shivered and drew his hand back from the door, clenching it into a fist as he stopped and gritted his teeth, trying to force the memory of his older brother Sirhan's death to go back where it belonged, into the deepest crevasses of his mind.

"It is not your fault, my dear Kabeer," the great Sheikh had told him in those royal chambers all those years ago, with the two queens on either side of him, Yasmeena at his feet, all of them somber and shaken, bereft and broken. "No one thinks it is your fault, and it is very important that *you*, my son, do not think it was your fault."

Of course it wasn't his fault. Not logically, at least. Kabeer knew it then and he knew it now. But emotionally . . . that was different. Emotionally that memory cut too deep to ever fully heal:

Princes Sirhan and Kabeer had been playing like boys play, running wild through those very same chambers of the Great Eastern Wing of the Royal Palace. They had been playing that old game called "Follow the Leader," and it was Kabeer's turn to lead.

Little Prince Kabeer was six years younger than Sirhan, but stood almost as tall and was certainly more athletic, and so Kabeer often attempted physically challenging acts when playing this particular game. The objective of "Follow the Leader" was to repeat what the leader had just done or else you lose, and Kabeer had just leapt from the top of one of those low wooden tables directly into a marble-lined fountain, landing on his feet in the ankle-deep water that was sprinkled with rose petals.

"Follow that, brother Sirhan!" Kabeer had squealed in Arabic as he bounded out of the fragrant water and stood to watch his brother make the leap.

But brother Sirhan was not endowed with the strong legs, the tall frame, the grace and agility of young Kabeer, and the older prince had tripped over the short marble wall of the fountain and tumbled head first into the fountain, hitting his head against the ornate marble centerpiece with such force that the sound of the deadly impact rang out through the open rooms, echoed off the high ceilings, tunneled its way into Kabeer's young mind, perhaps twisted its way into his psyche.

"I will never play that game again," little Kabeer had told his father that day as the Sheikh hugged his son while the women sat silently beside the Sheikh and his last remaining prince. "It is a dangerous game. No good can come of it. Father, I will never play Follow the Leader again!"

And Kabeer looked at his clenched fist and smiled, shaking his head as he felt those memories of his homeland and family recede to the background. Now he was that lone wolf again, and his territory was

American high-society, he reminded himself. A man answerable to no one. A leader of only himself, with no followers, no one to lead astray.

Then he knocked on the heavy wooden door, and in an exaggerated American accent that could not hide who he truly was, Kabeer Bukhaara called out, "It is me. Ready or not, I'm coming in."

8

Was she ready for this or not?

Jenny looked over and across the boundless lake. The wind was strong now, whipping her hair across her face just like it was stirring the great lake waters into thousands of white-tipped, ferocious little waves.

Are you ready, Jenny? Ready to navigate these waters that have gotten very complicated, very quickly? Ready to build the business that you've being dreaming about for years? Ready to risk your money, your time, your reputation on something that could wipe you out, use up that small inheritance, leave you bankrupt, jobless, with no chance of getting a real goddamn job because there's nothing on your resume except a part-time MBA and a full-time failed business?

Jenny turned and leaned back against the railing now, looking over the empty deck, now over at where Kabeer had been standing not so long ago. She had felt him there, standing quietly, watching her. She sensed him get close. She could almost feel his desire cut through the wild lake wind as he approached. And though she tried to make it stop, she could feel her own flames rise with his . . . yes, those flames of desire that licked at her secret depths like the wicked tongues of a thousand devils. She could feel the blood in her ears as the Sheikh took another step, and she had held that railing tight as she braced herself, prepared herself, readied herself . . .

Readied herself for what? Would she have told him to stop? Pushed him away? Turned him down? And would he have stopped? Would she have *wanted* him to stop?

Now *you* stop, she told herself as she crossed her arms over her chest and began to pace as a fever tore through her like that damned wind. Stop thinking yourself into circles. Stop mixing up what your body wants with what you know is the ultimate objective here: to figure out if it makes sense to sign this deal. If it makes *business* sense to sign this deal!

But how could she separate things now? Now that

Kabeer had demanded that *he* be the celebrity chef? And why the hell would he want to do it? Did he even know how to boil a goddamn egg? Could he even make himself mac-and-cheese out of a box if he had to? Celebrity . . . yes, Jenny could see that. If she— someone who never read celebrity news—had heard of him, it certainly meant something. And it wasn't like the celebrity that movie stars or hip-hop artists had—it was something more subtle, more secretive, more . . . exciting?

There you go again, she told herself, pacing down to the end of the deck and back again. She hugged herself and rocked back and forth as the thoughts and arguments, the pros and cons, the yays and nays fought and played, tussled and struggled, bitched and moaned, howled and groaned as everything played out in her head.

But it was no use, and as Jenny stepped to the railing again and looked down at the blue water zipping by, the frothy tops of little waves pointing and laughing at her like imps, she realized that she couldn't possibly sort it out cleanly. There were too many possibilities, too many potentials, too many ways this could go wrong . . . and a lot of ways this could go right. So right. Oh, *God*, so right!

Now the tension of the day made itself known once more, and she leaned over the side of the railing and just *screamed* into the wind, *wailed* up at the sky, and now she was laughing and crying, shivering and sweating, hot and cold, high and low, turned inside out, upside down, flipped over, twisted around, spun about like a top, and . . . and . . . and what do I do, what do I do, what do I *do*?!

Take the step and jump in, came that silent whisper, soft and silky through the roaring wind. Jump in, little Jenny. Yes, jump in and have faith that the universe will catch you.

Jump in.

9

"Look before you leap."

"What? I do not understand, Father."

"Look before you leap. The expression. You have heard it, Kabeer, yes?"

The old Sheikh raised his head from the cushioned end of the green-and-gold divan on which he lay. His right arm lay stretched out as an attendant sat on a wooden footstool beside him, taking the old man's blood pressure, it looked like.

"Yes, Father. I know the expression," Kabeer said, eyeing the black bag of medical paraphernalia that sat open on the long wooden table behind the attendant.

"Tell me what it means," the old Sheikh said now, wincing as the attendant tightened the blood pressure tube around his upper arm.

Kabeer sighed and rubbed the back of his neck. "What is this about, Father?"

The old Sheikh sighed too, but it was a different sort of sigh. While Kabeer's expression had been of impatience, the old man's was one of resignation, almost disappointment. Kabeer wasn't surprised—indeed, this was part of the reason for his impatience.

"I will answer my own question then," the Sheikh said as the blood pressure tube came off. The Sheikh waved the attendant away and then slowly propped himself up on a red silk cushion so he could face his son. "It means that one should understand what one is about to do before doing it. Do not jump before you know where you are going to land."

"Yes, Father," Kabeer said now, sighing again as he sat on a white leather couch across from the divan. He stretched out and exhaled. This was going to take a while. "I know what it means."

"I know you do," the Sheikh said, flashing a toothy grin. "I just wanted to make sure you knew this conversation is going to take a while."

Now Kabeer couldn't help but smile, and he raised his arms in defeat and sat up on the couch, leaning back and spreading his arms across the broad frame of the backrest. "Yasmeena has already talked to you," Kabeer said.

"Of course. In theory, I am the head of Bukhaara Capital. Yasmeena gives me all the details of every investment."

"Really," Kabeer said. "What did you think about that investment in Weston Technology from last year? Or was it Western Technology? Watson Technology? Remind me of the name again, Father. You know all the details, yes? Surely you remember the name of the company we put two hundred million dollars into last year."

Now it was the old Sheikh's turn to smile. "Fine," he said with a chuckle. "I have no idea what Bukhaara Capital invests in. Yes, when I travel to America I like to take some interest in what Yasmeena is doing with the company, and I offer my opinion on whatever deal she is currently looking at. But that is more for my amusement, and also because I know Yasmeena likes it when I take some interest in what she is doing with our businesses. Other than that, your sister is more than capable of handling the business, and I trust her completely. You, on the other hand . . ."

Kabeer's jaw tightened, his eyes turning a darker shade of green as he looked directly at his father. The old man was teasing, but not really teasing. It was his way, Kabeer knew. But Kabeer was no longer a child. He was a man. His own man. Yes, his own man, a man who would serve no master—certainly a man who would serve no country or its land, no people or their God.

Kabeer glanced at that collection of medical supplies that looked like a hospital stuffed into a goddamn briefcase, and then he looked up at his father again and spoke: "If this is yet another conversation about becoming Sheikh—"

But the old man cut him off. "*Becoming* Sheikh? Kabeer, you are *already* Sheikh! The title of Sheikh was yours the day you were born, by virtue of your royal blood! And a few years later, when your brother Sirhan died in that tragic accident, you became my heir and successor, the sole and rightful ruler of the country of our ancestors, the nation of our people, the land of our God." He paused now, swallowing and taking a breath. "The country of *your* ancestors. The nation of *your* people. The land of *your* God."

Kabeer crossed one leg over the other. His fingers tapped the hard frame of the leather couch. He wasn't going to take the bait this time, he told himself. He wasn't going to rise up and disavow the country of his birth, the small, rich nation founded by his own ancestors, strong, determined men and women of the same bloodline, the same blood that coursed through Kabeer's veins. He wasn't going to pretend that he didn't give a damn about his people, didn't recognize their warmth and charity, their need to live in a society that gave them freedom, justice, and safety while still respecting the holy laws of Allah and his prophets.

"Yasmeena is your eldest child," Kabeer said quietly. "She is your heir and successor. Allah knows she is capable. She has been running Bukhaara Capital for almost a decade now, negotiating complex business deals, analyzing all sorts of industries, managing the biggest—"

"And she will continue to do that," the Sheikh snapped now, his dark eyes moving back and forth, side to side as he searched his son's face like he was looking for something. "Managing billions of dollars of our family's—and our country's—money is a very serious and important job. And Yasmeena loves her work. It energizes her. Gives her purpose." Those eyes stopped darting back and forth now, and the old Sheikh held his gaze on his son. "Besides, the law is clear as written in the ancient scriptures, the law of our land. The eldest son is the true and rightful Sheikh. The *son*, Kabeer. You, Kabeer. *You!*"

Kabeer shrugged. "This is a new world. If you told any American woman that she could not be CEO or Senator or even President because she is a woman, then you would be called a sexist pig and—"

"My dear son, these days you would be called a sexist pig in Bukhaara as well if you said that! Still, Bukhaara is not America," the old Sheikh said, his tone betraying the effort he was making to keep his voice somewhat calm. "Yes, there are many things I love and admire about this country, including the freedom that women have to find their own paths, pursue their own goals without being restricted by outdated or oppressive laws. And you know quite well that I have changed many of Bukhaara's laws to make sure our country's women are given equal place in society, power in their marriage, freedom to pursue any sort of education or occupation. But there are certain traditions that cannot be broken. Certain traditions that *will* not be broken. Not in my time, at least." Now he found some calm, and the Sheikh's breathing slowed as he smiled at his son. "And your sister agrees with me."

Kabeer shifted on his seat now. Certainly, Yasmeena had often been vocal, pushy, and—like today in her room—almost insulting in the way she challenged him, almost dared him to step up and take over as Sheikh of Bukhaara. But Kabeer had always shrugged it off, never taken it too seriously. He had told her point blank many times that he had no interest in being Sheikh and that in fact she would be a very capable Sheikha. He had told her he would support her, support any change in laws that needed to happen. And although she had laughed it off, claiming to be happy running Bukhaara Capital and traveling the world looking for new companies to invest in, Kabeer had always suspected that she was simply waiting for her father to say the word. And once he did, Kabeer thought as he glanced at his father and nodded, then Yasmeena would drop everything in a heartbeat, put on that veil that she always hated, and become Sheikha without a second thought, without looking back.

"Of course Yasmeena agrees with you," Kabeer said, smiling as he pointed out what to him was obvious, had always been obvious. "She is Daddy's girl when it comes down to it. She will always agree with you. And if you ask her to be Sheikha, she will do it without a moment's—"

"I have already asked her," the old Sheikh said quietly, leaning back into the silk cushions of the divan, exhaling as he relaxed his thin, wiry frame. "She will not do it. She says you will be a better Sheikh. The people will respond to you better. They will follow you in a way they will not follow her."

Now Kabeer laughed in disbelief, wondering for a moment if his father's physical ailments had spread to his brain—or at least his hearing. "Yasmeena said that? She said I am better suited to lead our nation than she is? I do not believe it."

"She said it herself, I assure you," the old man said, looking up at the ornate blue-and-pink painted ceiling and shaking his head, an affectionate smile coming to his thin lips. "Yasmeena is smart and self-aware. In some ways she is wiser than both of us put together. She understands that the job of Sheikh is to lead the people in spirit more than anything. Some of the most important work of a Sheikh in today's world is public relations. There will be speeches, exhibitions, opening ceremonies of museums and sports arenas. Television appearances, radio interviews, photographs taken every day, from every angle. Your every move will be watched, photographed, and then commented on throughout the region." Now the Sheikh looked over at his son, his old eyes suddenly looking sharp, focused. "Does that sound more like your world or Yasmeena's world, Kabeer?"

Kabeer was silent as his thoughts raced. He could not argue the point. His father was right, and Yasmeena—if she had indeed said those things—was right too. Yasmeena was intelligent and driven, but she had little patience when it came to things she considered unnecessary and ceremonial. She rarely posed for photographs. She never celebrated her birthday. She seemed to have no interest in marriage, of raising a family. There was not a romantic or sentimental bone in her body, it seemed sometimes!

Now Kabeer blinked several times and shook his head as he realized what was happening. His father was smart, wise, and yes: crafty as all hell! The old man was slowly pulling him in, Kabeer realized as he felt a distant swell of emotion from that place deep inside, the place where all those old memories of Bukhaara were hidden, the place from which those annoying emotions like duty, honor, courage kept bubbling up when he thought about his supposed responsibility to be Sheikh of Bukhaara.

"You cannot run from your destiny forever," the old Sheikh said now as he watched his son. "That is the definition of destiny in a way—something that will find you no matter which way you turn!" Now his voice dropped to a whisper. "And the funny thing is, sometimes when it seems you are running away from your destiny, in fact you are running straight towards it."

Now the Sheikh closed his eyes and snapped his fingers, and two attendants came out of seemingly nowhere. One of them was wheeling in a medical drip-stand. The other began preparing a syringe from the medical supplies on the table. It was time to go, Kabeer knew. His father had—like he always did— ended the conversation on his own terms.

Kabeer stormed out of the room, his insides twisted and knotted from the conflicting emotions that threatened to rip him apart. He did not want to acknowledge them. They were like little demons living in his head, and the moment he gave them some attention, they would take over, he decided. So shut them down, Kabeer. Stay on the path you have chosen. Your father is wrong. Yasmeena is wrong. You are a lone wolf, not a leader of a nation of people looking for a damn role model.

Yes, you are a lone wolf, Kabeer thought as he summoned up the image of that curvy American woman who had gotten him so close to what he knew would bring him the peace he needed right now.

A lone wolf, he muttered as that image of Jenny's smooth, pretty face, her big brown eyes, those magnificent contours flashed in his mind as he stormed up to the deck. He imagined her standing there against the railing, her full figure on display in the sunlight, her hair wild and flying like a battle flag, calling to him.

I'm coming, Jenny Jones. Ready or not, I'm coming.

10

"**I**'ve succeeded at every damned thing I've put my mind to, Jenny," Kabeer said as he ran his fingers through his thick, dark brown hair. "My sister is not a fool. There is no way she'd have agreed to let me do this if she did not think I could pull it off."

"And when is someone going to ask for *my* opinion when it comes to, you know, *my* restaurant?!" Jenny was red in the face, her hands shaking as she reached for the glass of water an attendant had just brought up on a tray.

They were still on that upper deck, sitting on a white linen couch that faced the back of the boat.

Kabeer had burst up onto the deck a few minutes earlier, his dark face flush, his green eyes sharp and focused . . . focused on her.

Oh, God, she had thought for a moment as he approached. She could smell it on him, his desire, his need, his want. And she could feel it in herself again too, like her body was choosing to respond immediately to his, like they were already in tune, in rhythm, in sync. She tried not to look down, and in truth she did not need to, because there was no doubt that he was ready to take what he wanted.

A part of her wanted to give in right then and there. Jump in, right? But just as the Sheikh drew near, Jenny felt the boat change direction. She looked towards the horizon, where she could see the glass and steel towers of Chicago shimmering in the sun. Sure enough, the boat was turning. They were heading back. The clock was ticking. Jenny needed to give Yasmeena her answer.

She already knew that she'd sign that offer sheet— she really had no choice. But she still couldn't make complete sense of the Sheikh's strange demand to be head chef. It couldn't be just about the "experience," could it? He was a billionaire! He could open ten restaurants in Paris, play around in the kitchens, and close them down if he got bored! But it couldn't be just because of her either, she had decided. If Kabeer just wanted to sleep with her, wouldn't it be easier for a man like that to *not* volunteer to work closely with her every day for months, maybe longer?! What was this man trying to do? What was he trying to get?

And so instead of listening to her body, Jenny tried to shut it up, close it down, turn it off. She walked past the Sheikh as he approached her with that look on his face, and she quickly sat on that white couch, crossing a leg over the other, folding her arms tightly over her breasts. We're going to talk, she told herself. This is still a damned business meeting, as far as I'm concerned. Isn't it?

So she had started to talk, but the tone was heated, passionate, tense and dramatic as their shared arousal colored every sentence, underlined every word, heightened every emotion. And then, before she knew it, Jenny was red in the face and saying:

"And when is someone going to ask for *my* opinion when it comes to, you know, *my* restaurant?!"

Kabeer laughed as he took a seat right beside her, very close, too damned close maybe. "You are not a fool either, Jenny. You know that Bukhaara Capital will be the majority owner of your company once you sign that term sheet. That's how venture capital works. My family is bringing the money, and we have the final say in how this business is run. This is how it is going to be." He paused now, touching his lips and looking at her in a way that almost made her uncomfortable, certainly made her shift in her seat, perhaps loosen up her posture just a bit. "And you know what, Jenny? It just occurred to me that you—innocent brown eyes and all—would *never* be able to work with an actual celebrity chef, someone who already has a culinary style and reputation, years of training and experience. Ya, Allah, no damned way! Oh, I already see it! You have too strong a belief in your own vision! You are so determined, so focused, so clear on what you want this to be that it's . . . it's . . . it's goddamn intoxicating."

And he just leaned over and kissed her, hard on the lips, his right hand grazing her cheek as he firmly gripped her hair just above the back of her neck, grasping down near the roots and pulling as he forced his tongue into her mouth.

"Kabeer!" she gurgled as she felt a wave of panicked ecstasy *rip* through her as she opened her mouth and let him in, let him kiss her full, kiss her hard, kiss her the way he wanted, kiss her the way *she* wanted.

He gripped the back of her neck now as they kissed, his hand moving down along her upper arm, massaging her flesh so hard it made her groan. That hand on her hip now, her thighs, already trying to push her legs apart, slide in there, deep in there where she could feel her wetness once more. Perhaps it had never gone away.

"Kabeer," she said again, but this time it was a whisper as she touched his face, ran her hands along his stubble, touched his full, dark red lips with her thumbs and forefingers, looked into his deep green eyes. "What is happening? Oh, God, what's happening?"

Kabeer pulled away and abruptly stood up. He was panting hard, smiling wide, his thick hair mussed from the way Jenny had clawed at it when he kissed her like that . . . kissed her without warning, without permission, just because he damned well wanted.

And now as she looked up at Kabeer standing in the sun before her, unbuttoning his crisp white shirt until it hung open all the way down, six-pack abs looking tight and bronze, like they were shrink-wrapped and polished as that shirt flew like a flag in the wind . . . yes, now, as the sun hit this man from behind, casting his body in a million little shadows that made her toes curl up . . . yes, she got a strange image of him standing in the desert, a sandstorm at his back, that white shirt looking like a flowing white caftan as it billowed in the storm winds. He looked like a king for that strange moment, like something out of an old story, something out of the past . . . perhaps something out of the future . . . something out of *their* future . . .

And then, as he changed position, coming closer to her as she looked up at him, she once again saw his modern trousers, his collared shirt, those rock-star good looks and that killer grin. Who is this man, she wondered. Which image is the right one? Is he Sheikh

Kabeer Bukhaara, leader of his ancestral homeland, or is he just K.B., international billionaire. Was there a depth to him that she was refusing to see even though some part of her was begging to acknowledge it. Or was this just her frazzled brain getting twisted and turned by the blaze of the sun, the heat of arousal.

The heat of arousal, Jenny thought as she became eminently conscious of her wetness seeping through her panties and tights now as she caught Kabeer glancing at her chest, the swell of her breasts beneath that jacket. And now the sun felt very hot as she shifted on that linen couch, and she could feel perspiration along her arms as her breathing became labored. Kabeer's shirt was off now, and he looked so damned hot, his flat stomach and rock-hard chest exposed, those thick veins like ropes circling his arms, that grin that had gotten her wet twice today already. And now she felt dizzy as the unsatisfied arousal began to bubble up so hard it scared her, and she blinked and looked away and then up once more at the Sheikh as he towered above her, almost blocking out the sun.

"You look warm in that suit, Jenny," Kabeer said, his grin widening as he leaned over the low table and reached for her. "Here. Let me."

Jenny's arms were still folded across her chest, and Kabeer held her wrists and slowly, with overwhelming strength, pried her arms apart and raised them up and to the sides, pinning them across the back of the couch as he leaned in and kissed her full, gently but with absolute power, focused intent.

He held her arms pinned down to her side as they kissed, and then he let go. She looked up at him as she licked her lips. She did not move her arms back across her chest, and now she shivered and blinked, exhaled quickly as he pulled her jacket open, inhaled sharply as he touched the tips of her breasts through her top and bra, teasing her nipples with the back of his rough hands before gently pinching them to hardness through the cloth.

"I want to take this off," he whispered as he pushed the low table away from her and then sat on it, his hands gripping the lapels of her jacket. He touched her breasts again now, drawing a whimper from Jenny as she felt electricity zip through her hot body as her nipples responded quickly. Then he pulled at her jacket again. "This is in my way. It comes off now. Now, Jenny. Come on."

Kabeer pulled her forward and she let him slip the jacket off her. He tossed it onto the chair behind him. Now he reached down for the bottom of her black top, pulling it up over her breasts firmly, with authority, no hesitation.

"Oh, God, Kabeer. We're outside! What are you doing?!" she whispered as she gasped at the heat of the sun hitting her exposed skin, her bare stomach, the top of her breasts that were bursting out of her bra, her bra that felt very tight and uncomfortable right now, like it needed to come off right now, right now, ohgod right now . . .

"You ask too many questions," Kabeer muttered as his strong hands closed tight on her breasts, squeezing hard as Jenny arched her back and moaned involuntarily.

The sturdy couch creaked as Kabeer knelt down and leaned in, pushing her legs apart with his body as he began to kiss her furiously, pinching her nipples through her bra. She gasped and tilted her head back as he moved down to her neck. Her eyes were clamped shut, everything looking red as the sun warmed her upturned face. She felt Kabeer massage her naked upper arms as he licked her neck, now grasping her wrists and raising her arms above her head as he kissed her cleavage, sucked her nipples through the sheer black bra, soaking the thin cloth with his warm saliva.

"Kabeer, we're out in the open," she whispered, but she didn't stop him as he slid his tongue between the globes of her breasts, his hands up her skirt, fingers digging into her thighs and bottom through her tights. "Someone's going to come up here."

"Nobody will come up here," Kabeer rasped in her ear as he gently pulled on her earlobe with his teeth, his hand caressing her bare neck, squeezing once and then letting go. He kissed her on the lips again, gently now, carefully, his eyes looking into hers. His hand moved down to her breast again, and he lowered her bra-cup and gasped as his fingers closed on her stiff, rock-hard nipple. "And if they do, it means nothing. I do not give a damn, and neither should you. We are not stopping for anything. For anyone. This is happening, Jenny Jones. Right here. Right now. No goddamn questions. Your body has already answered the only damned question that is relevant right now." He looked down at her creamy white breasts, the nipples pert and hard, dark pink and proud in the sun. "Oh, God, Jenny. I am so bloody hot for you. So damned hard for you. Come here."

And now he stood up off that low table, pulling her off the couch with all his strength, and she was breathless as she slammed against his hard body. He held her tight as he whipped around and *kicked* one of those heavy deck chairs out of the way, sending it tumbling along the wooden deck, colorful striped cushions flying everywhere. He kissed her face again, his warm lips exploring every inch of her smooth skin—her cheeks, her nose, her lips, her chin, her forehead, even her eyelids as she blinked and moaned under his touch.

His strong hands were squeezing her ass with tremendous force, pulling her cheeks apart even through her tights and skirt. Fingers clawing at the expanse of her bottom, now hands moving down to the hem of her skirt, pulling upwards, hiking up her skirt over her ass now, all the way up to her hips. Those long fingers running down along her rear crack now, pushing their way underneath, between her legs from behind, teasing her most secret space from beneath as she wriggled and moved.

Now Kabeer's hands moved up to her waist and found the top of her tights, quickly sliding in, down into her tight black panties, fingers spreading and clutching fistfuls of her naked ass. The sensation of his fingers on her skin was raw, sensual, goddamn *wild*, and Jenny felt her own wetness against her inner thighs as Kabeer slowly pushed her panties and tights down even as he caressed every inch of her round buttocks.

"But your sister . . ." Jenny muttered as she felt the warm breeze against her bare ass and thighs and realized that her panties and tights were almost down to her knees. "Kabeer, your sister said . . ."

Kabeer pulled back his head and blinked as he stared at her. "Why the hell is my sister relevant right now? Are you insane?"

"No," Jenny shuddered as she exhaled. "Before she left she warned me that I'd need to learn how to keep my personal feelings separate from my business relationships, and—"

But she couldn't finish the sentence, because just as she spoke Kabeer touched her with the back of his hand, touched her right down there, right in front, and it sent a shudder through her as he rubbed her with the back of his hand, his knuckle grazing her clit, his finger reaching out and tracing its way lengthwise against her slit that was so wet, so wet, so *damned* wet right now.

"Listen to me, Jenny Jones," he whispered hungrily as his fingers slowly teased the edges of her slit until she could literally feel it opening up for him, "we are not in business together until you sign that offer sheet. So right now, this here . . . this is one-hundred-percent personal. One hundred percent personal. Just you and me. Man and woman. Man and woman. And right now, right here, you are my woman. *My* damn woman."

And he slid his middle finger into her as he said it, his thumb resting on her clit as his middle finger drove deep and smooth, and she almost choked in ecstasy as he gently curled that thick, long finger up inside her, and he was controlling her with that finger, owning her with his thumb, ruling her with his touch.

They stood there in the sun, bodies pressed against each other, him kissing her on the lips, tongue pushing inside her just like his fingers were inside her, and she muttered as he worked her, moaned as he tasted her, shuddered as he tapped his thumb against her.

The orgasm came silently, sneaking up on her like a tornado in the night, and she gagged and flailed as she came, convulsed as the full force of that orgasm hit, swooned as he held her close, his fingers still and motionless inside her as she exhaled in short, gasping, desperate breaths as the ecstasy took over her senses one by one until the only sensation left was touch. The feeling of him touching her.

11

The sun and the sky, the water and the wind, the boat, the waves, the view . . . all of it disappeared into the background as Kabeer kissed her lips, touched her body, caressed her curves. She was overwhelming him in a way he had never experienced—not with European supermodels, South American popstars, Asian beauty queens, or American millionaire-princesses. And it wasn't just her body—it was everything. The way she carried herself. That hint of self-doubt and insecurity that existed side-by-side with a deep faith in herself, a real inner strength, the kind of strength that made her challenge herself, to move forward even when she was scared.

Kabeer had always been good at reading people, and although he knew he was right about her so far, he also knew that there was so much to this woman that he didn't have a clue about yet, that he would still need to discover . . . and *damn* it was going to be a fun journey of discovery. Yes, suddenly he wanted to experience every part of her—mind and body, inside and outside, soul and spirit. Just like his tongue was exploring her smooth skin, just like his fingers were seeking her secret spaces, just like his eyes were looking into hers, looking for . . . looking for . . . looking for what?

Love?

Am I insane?

The thought struck him as he felt Jenny come in his arms, under his deep touch, her body thrashing and shivering as he held her close, held her tight, held her like he had known her for years, held her like she was his.

Like she was his.

He felt so damn close to her as she came. He could feel her hot breath against his chest as she gasped and sputtered her way to that silent climax. It made him feel connected to her in a way that was so much deeper than his fingers curling inside her secret depths.

This is not a woman who gives herself easily, Kabeer said to himself as she finally opened her eyes and gazed up at him with those big brown eyes that looked just a bit hazy right now as she whimpered and blinked. Even when I first saw her I thought she was unlike so many other American women whose names and faces all blend into one meaningless set of events that suddenly seem to be in the distant past. And now I can only confirm what my body was telling me when I first touched her curves in that dark, silent underground garage, those black limousines our only witnesses. Allah knows I have been with enough women to instantly sense when something is different, when *someone* is different. And this one is different. Oh, God help me, she is different.

Do you know it, little Jenny? he wondered as he smiled down at her blushing round face, her genuine modesty perhaps breaking through and reminding her that she was half naked on the open deck of a boat, that a man she had met three hours ago had just made her come hard and was holding her now, looking at her with all the intensity he had, all the passion he had. All of it.

Do you know how different this feels for me? he wondered again as he touched her hair, gently teasing open a series of loose knots that the wind had lovingly tied into her thick brown tresses.

No, he decided as he kissed her forehead. You do not know, and perhaps even I do not know. Perhaps it is just that I am going temporarily mad from the arousal and I just need to—

"Oh, Kabeer," Jenny whispered as she looked down along his naked chest and abs, her hand reaching for the hardness that was pushing against the front of his trousers, pushing against the cloth and making his crotch so tight it hurt. "You're so hard."

All thoughts vanished like smoke in the night, and Kabeer grunted and shuddered out a smile as he took her soft hand and guided it firmly around the outline of his cock. He shuddered again as he felt her fingers close hard around his girth, his muscles tensing up as he pressed his body into hers where they stood.

"Ya, Allah," he muttered into her hair as she pulled at his cock, slowly and firmly going back and forth through the cloth. "I need that. I need it."

He undid his belt as she worked him, his groans and pants increasing as she pulled harder, his fingers shaking as he undid the top button of his fitted black trousers that were straining at the seams from his bulging need. Now he pushed back and unzipped, letting the silky smooth trousers drop all the way to the polished wooden deck. He stepped out of the crumpled cloth, looking down at the peaked tower in his black Italian underwear.

He was about to push his underwear down when Jenny was back against him, her body slamming against his so quickly it surprised him, aroused him, got him harder, hard as hell. Now she slipped her warm hand down the front of his underwear as he furiously kissed her lips, pushing his tongue into her mouth with desperation as he felt her fingers find their way around his swollen girth.

"Oh, God, Kabeer," she gurgled as he kissed her harder. "Here. Let me——"

She began to pull his underwear down over his tight hips, lowering herself to the deck floor as she did it, but Kabeer grabbed her tight around the upper arms and shook his head firmly.

"No," he said. "That is not what I want right now."

He pulled back from her and strode quickly to where a set of thick red towels were neatly folded in a stack, and he grabbed two and opened them up. The red cloth billowed in the wind as he shook them open and then placed them on the brown boards of the smooth wooden deck.

"Come here," he said, his jaw set as he reached for her hand. "Down."

She hesitated for a moment, but just a moment, and now his arm was around her naked waist. A swift kiss—hard and raw like he meant it—and then Kabeer had pulled her half-lowered tights and panties all the way down to her ankles as he helped her sit on the soft towels.

He could smell her as he pulled the tights and panties off her feet and flung them over his head, gasping as the warm, clean aroma of her sex came to him in a rush that made him dizzy with need. Ya, Allah, she smelled so good. Smelled like a woman. Like his woman.

"Keep the bra strap on," he ordered as he squeezed her breasts once more before pushing her down onto her back and then raising her bra cups, releasing the full globes of her soft white breasts. "I like how your bra looks pushed up over your breasts, your nipples sticking up like pink domes, peaked like minarets."

Jenny's tongue darted out and curled up over her top lip, and her neck arched back as Kabeer pressed his fully naked, rock-hard body down on top of hers, running his tongue up her neck, to her lips, into her mouth, licking her face now as he felt his cock naturally push against the delicate clump of hair covering the front of her sex, forcing her legs open as it sought her secret opening.

His underwear was still on, wet with his fresh pre-cum, and he went back on his knees and pushed them down, immediately releasing his heavy, full, engorged cock.

"Oh, *God*, Kabeer," Jenny gasped as she looked down past herself at his thick cock, brown and heavy, the monstrous shaft wet with his own fluids, the swollen head dark red and glistening in the sunlight.

She hunched over now, reaching for him, his hardness, and Kabeer grimaced in ecstasy as she stroked the underside of his cock, her other hand massaging his heavy balls as he stayed suspended above her, looking down at her. She looked so bloody hot from above—her smooth round face contorted with desire, her magnificent breasts pressed together as she hunched up, that delicate triangle of brown hair shielding her sex in a feminine way that was bringing him close to orgasm already.

His eyes glazed over as he took in the sight of her shaking body, naked and smooth, her curves glistening in the sunshine. Her nipples were bright red and stiff like bullets standing on end, and he lowered himself and sucked hard on each one as he teased the top of her slit with his swollen tip. She shook and shivered as he ran the broad, oozing head of his cock along her slit lengthwise, slowly opening her up. Oh, God, she is so warm, he thought. So wet. So damned perfect.

He shuddered as he felt her vagina open up for him as he pushed, slowly but with power, reveling in the feeling of every inch sliding into Jenny as her inner walls pressed tightly against his girth. He could feel her breathe below him, her chest pushing against his as he pressed his body slowly against her and drove his throbbing shaft all the way up inside her, flexing his cock as he felt Jenny take the final inch of his hardness deep into her warm valleys.

But then, "Kabeer," she whispered from below him, her hand firm against his chest now, holding him back. "We should—"

"No," he growled as he began to move inside her,

flexing his cock again as he felt the walls of her vagina so damn tight against his girth. "You are so wet, Jenny. By God, I can smell you. I can feel your wetness dripping onto my balls. I can damn near *taste* you. Do not *dare* tell me to stop right now!"

"Oh, God, no, I want this," she whispered. "But not without—"

"I will pull out before I finish," he muttered now, panting as he began to thrust, groaning as he felt her heat, her wetness, her need. "Do not worry, little Jenny. It will be fine. Come. Come now. Here we go. There we go. Oh, God, Jenny. You are so soft, so wet, so hot inside, so damned tight inside."

So tight, he thought as he felt his mouth hang open with ecstasy as he began to drive deep into her dark depths under the bright sunshine. So tight, and so goddamn right.

Ya Allah, he thought as he closed his eyes and took her deep, took her bare, took her hard. So goddamn right.

12

Jenny almost choked in ecstasy as she felt Kabeer's tremendous girth stretch her wide, *so* wide, and her mouth opened involuntarily in a silent scream as she felt his hardness fill her up so rapidly that her eyes rolled up in her head every time he flexed his shaft. He moved slowly but firmly, pushed with gentleness but power, his length driving deep even as his thick shaft filled her so completely she could feel him against every inch of her inner walls. It was like he was made for her, she thought in a crazy moment as she felt him push deeper, deeper, so *goddamn* deep.

I trust him, she told herself as she felt the ecstasy radiate outwards from her core. I trust him even though I have no reason to trust him, even though I have every reason *not* to trust him.

But that inner voice was drowned out in a moment, that same moment when she felt him flex again inside her, the upward curve of his cock making her groan and hunch up and into him as he drew back and then pushed into her again, thrusting slowly, slowly, slowly . . . speeding up but still slow, moving faster now, rotating his powerful hips as he pushed back in, his hand sliding behind the curve of her back, pulling her body up as her head tilted back, and he *drove* inside again, drawing back long and coming in full again, taking her nipple in his mouth now, him sucking so hard it damn near hurt, but it felt so good, so deep, so raw, so *right*.

"*Awha, alllaha, wahadha hu mithl alhulm,*" he muttered as his head drew back from her arched chest, a long trail of clean saliva connecting his lower lip to her shining nipple. "*Waqalat 'annaha alihat fi alhulim, hu 'annaha la?*"

The Arabic sounded strange, smooth, exotic and erotic, and Jenny smiled and closed her eyes as she focused on his deep voice, the strange language adding to her arousal as the Sheikh moved faster inside, pushed himself so deep she called out in surprise, her own voice sounding strange and foreign now, and she was tightening her legs around him, bucking her hips into him as he *rammed* his body down on her now, and she was gasping as his weight pressed down on her, moaning as his length pushed into her, and they were in rhythm now, their naked bodies sweating in the blazing sun, the heat inside her matching the heat outside, and Kabeer pumped his powerful hips as Jenny bucked and flailed, and then suddenly, without warning, with a roaring cry of "Ya, Allah!" Kabeer *exploded* inside her, *shouting* as he came, *roaring* as he poured his heat into her depths, and before the panic had any chance to rise up, before she had time to even understand what had happened, out of nowhere her own orgasm *screamed* in like a runaway train in the night, and suddenly they were coming together, coming *hard*, both of them clutching at each other, sounds like wild animals emerging from their fierce embrace, and the sun was blasting down on them as they climaxed in unison, their cries merging with the screams of the gulls, the howl of the wind, the roar of the waves.

They came together, and no one knows how long they shuddered and groaned, shivered and moaned against one another, and their shared climax could have lasted an hour, a day, their entire goddamn lives. Time slowed down and sped up as Jenny's orgasms rolled in like that night-train derailing at breakneck speed, the waves of ecstasy rocking her body, sending convulsions through her as she felt the Sheikh come deep inside her, his semen pouring into her depths as she felt his heavy balls slap against her skin with every powerful thrust.

It felt like eternity and Jenny wanted it to last eternity, but the peak was too high to sustain, and soon she shuddered and shook her way down through a series of secondary orgasms as she felt Kabeer flex again inside her one last time, his final discharge making her whimper as she felt him flood her secret canals, filling every corner of her depths like it was a dream.

"Oh, God," she whispered, her chest heaving as she felt hot and wet all over, sweat mixing with everything else. "Oh, *God*, Kabeer!"

"Oh, no, no, *no*!" Kabeer shouted. He pulled out with a groan and rolled off her and onto the red towels on which they lay. He panted as he lay on his back, and squinted up at the bright blue sky. But then almost immediately he turned and pulled her close again, wrapping her up with his warm, hard body, his face close to hers, chest heaving, lips moving in wet silence against her warm, wet cheek. "Do not think," he whispered. "Do not talk. No thinking. No talking. Just stop everything. Come here. Come to me. Be close."

Jenny stayed silent as she listened to the waves and the wind. She was still in that dream, that dream where she could hear herself whimper and sob like it was another person making those sounds, some other girl who had slipped into her body. She closed her eyes and did what he said: tried not to think.

Yes, she closed her eyes and let the world spin on outside, like she and Kabeer were not part of the real world right now. The thought comforted her, and in a moment of madness she decided that this was indeed a dream, and logic and common sense meant nothing in this fantasy world.

She kept her eyes shut tight for a long time, breathing deeply, taking in Kabeer's masculine smell, the dusky smell of his cologne mixing with the aroma of their combined sweat, their combined sex. And when she finally fluttered her eyelids and tried to blink away the tears that she didn't even know had come, she was greeted with the strangest of gazes from the greenest of eyes.

What is that I see in his eyes, she wondered as she felt the sun warm her shoulders and face. Is it panic? Fear? Surprise? Is it an apology? Or is it something else?

Then it came to her. It wasn't so much what she saw in his eyes. It was what she didn't see.

And she didn't see panic. She didn't see fear. She didn't see surprise. She sure as hell didn't see an apology, or any indication that it had been a mistake.

Was it a mistake, she wondered now as her own panic began to tear down those pathways vacated by ecstasy. Was it a mistake, she wondered again, unable to speak and instead just searching those exotic green eyes for answers.

Yes, *was* it a mistake, great Sheikh?!

13

"**Y**es, Great Sheikh. I understand. I shall do my best, Inshallah. Rest now. Rest, dear Father."

Yasmeena quietly pulled the heavy wooden door closed behind her as she stepped out of her father's rooms below decks. She felt an unusual swell of emotion as she took that last look at her old father gingerly lie down on the green-and-gold divan. The old Sheikh was to head back to Bukhaara in three days, but he had just informed her he would be leaving tonight. Yasmeena did not ask why. She knew why.

He needed to go home. He needed to go home, because he could not—he *would* not—die in any other place.

She hadn't said goodbye. Hadn't said farewell. She did not cry. She would not cry. It was not her way, and it was not her family's way. Death was a part of life, and Yasmeena knew this as well as anyone—indeed, she had already lost a brother, a mother, a step-mother, and it was clear that life does not stop and give you time to grieve.

So she listened to her father's last set of instructions, and she nodded like a faithful daughter, a loyal princess, a woman who knew that her responsibilities were great—responsibilities to a family, a nation, a people, a way of life. Her father was trusting her to bring about something that she was not sure she could accomplish, but that was not an excuse not to try. And try she would.

Now Yasmeena walked to her cabin and sat at the teakwood table. She closed her eyes and meditated on what her father, the old Sheikh of Bukhaara, had asked her to do. In a way she did not have to do anything, she realized as she focused on her own breathing. Things would take their course. Kabeer would have no real choice to make. Once her father was gone, how could Kabeer choose to live in America when he was to be crowned Sheikh and ruler of his ancestral homeland, leader of his people? No, he would return to the Middle-East, to Bukhaara, to his homeland, his people, his duty. He could not choose to stay in America. No, of course not! There is nothing here he cannot have in Bukhaara. He will make the right choice.

Yes, but what if he does not, Yasmeena thought as a nagging doubt emerged along with an image of that full-figured woman that Kabeer had chosen to bring to a private family meeting—something Kabeer *never* did. No, that would never . . . it would never . . . it would never . . . it will not.

Ya, Allah, it will *not*!

14

Kabeer Bukhaara tapped his fingers on the smooth wooden desk. He was waiting for Yasmeena, and though ordinarily he would have been annoyed at being kept waiting, right now he didn't care. His mind was elsewhere. By God, all of him was elsewhere—mind, body, and spirit.

Jenny hadn't taken his calls for a week, and she hadn't replied to his messages. Kabeer was surprised, even angry. He could not remember the last time a woman hadn't responded to him. What was with this woman? What the hell was she up to?

Was she angry about how the sex ended? Worried

that she might be pregnant? Perhaps. Even I should be worried, should I not? he thought as he glanced at an old photograph on Yasmeena's office wall, almost hidden from clear sight unless you were sitting behind her desk. The picture was of the Bukhaara royal family—not one of the hundreds of posed photographs taken by professionals, but an informal picture taken with a camera set on a timer. Kabeer remembered that day—All three children, both queens, the Sheikh, and no one else! Just the family on a Sunday afternoon!

Kabeer blinked and turned away from the photograph and back to his thoughts. Yes, why was he not worried about Jenny being pregnant? God, it would be a disaster in a hundred ways, would it not? But if he could replay that moment, would he do anything different? Ya, Allah, he knew he would not! No, he would relive that moment a thousand times if he could, relive it exactly the same way, Jenny and him so close together, like they were one person, one body, one soul, one life, one universe even, all on their own. The sex was transcendent, the moment resplendent. In a way time had stopped for him at that very moment of their shared climax, and time was still frozen, like he had stepped into eternity, stepped into eternity with this American woman with those big brown eyes and those full pink lips and curves that made the Earth spin faster for Kabeer.

Did she feel this way? Like it was something more

than just sex? Perhaps this woman does not have the sexual history I do, he wondered now as he realized that it had only been one goddamn day with her and they still knew nothing about each other. Yes, perhaps she does not realize how unusual, how rare, how unique it is to feel a connection like this between two bodies, an unspoken connection that almost *has* to be otherworldly, for no explanation can be found for it in this world!

But Jenny did not say anything about it on the boat the rest of that trip. In fact, she did not say much of anything the rest of that trip, Kabeer thought. I offered to take her home, but she politely said she would take a taxi. I would have laughed and grabbed her and tied her to my damn motorcycle if we were alone, but with Yasmeena and Father and a thousand attendants, I had to be at least somewhat civilized. But ya Allah, I cannot stay civilized around this woman much longer. Where is she?!

"Ah, Kabeer, yes," Yasmeena's voice rang out as he heard her brisk footsteps in the hallway behind him. "Let us get started."

"No apology?" Kabeer said, remaining seated with one leg crossed over the other knee as Yasmeena walked around the desk and looked at him with surprise.

"For what?" she said.

"You are late. I do not tolerate late."

Yasmeena blinked as she looked at her brother. Her mouth opened like she was about to reply, but then she raised her right hand, shook her head as if to clear it, placed both hands on the table, and looked Kabeer right in the eye. "I am sorry, brother. There. OK now?"

"What do you want, Yasmeena? I have things to do," Kabeer growled, looking at his phone again as he scrolled for new messages. There were scores of new messages—like there always were—but nothing from Jenny.

"It is not what I want, Kabeer. This meeting is about what you want."

Kabeer looked up from his phone now. "And what is that?"

"Jenny Jones," said Yasmeena, sitting down and leaning back.

Kabeer glowered and almost crushed his phone as he clenched. "What about her?"

"You have slept with her."

"It is none of your damned business, Yasmeena."

Yasmeena shook her head, thought for a moment, and then shrugged. "Fine. Whatever may or may not have happened between you and her on the boat is indeed your business. But she has signed our offer sheet, and Bukhaara Capital has allocated her funds. We are in business with Jenny Jones now, and so from now on it *is* my business. And yours too, dear brother. It is *all* business now." She snorted, shaking her head. "Especially now that you have committed to this ridiculous idea of being head chef. Ay, *Khodai*! Do you ever think before doing things anymore? If you want to just back off and drop this idea, it would be good. Think about it."

Kabeer stayed quiet. Although all his intelligence and common sense told him he should back off, for some reason he felt more determined than ever. "It is not going to be a problem," he said after a moment.

"Kabeer, listen, if you are serious about this head chef position—"

"You know I am serious about it, Yasmeena. I do not make a lot of commitments, but when I do, I damned well follow through. You know that, Yasmeena. You *know* that!"

Yasmeena looked up in surprise at Kabeer's outburst. She searched his face for a moment, her gray eyes examining her brother's expression like she was trying to read something in it. Or perhaps she was considering her next words—Kabeer could not tell.

Now Yasmeena abruptly blinked and looked away and nodded. "Yes. OK. Then Kabeer, you must understand that you *cannot* be romantically linked with Jenny once we get started. Do you understand why?"

Kabeer was silent once again as he realized where his sister was going with this. Ordinarily he would have figured it out too—he was as sharp a business mind as she was. But his judgment was clouded, he knew. Clouded by what he could only describe as *feelings* for this woman, this woman who had invaded his mind in just one goddamn day!

Yasmeena continued. "Yes, Kabeer? You understand that once we begin the public relations campaigns, if the press picks up that there is *anything* going on between you and Jenny, they will immediately spin it as—"

"As if my family company is funding her restaurant because I am sleeping with her," Kabeer said with an uncharacteristic waver in his voice. "It would kill her credibility immediately. Make her look like she didn't get funded on the merits of her idea and her talent. Make her look like a . . . like a . . ." He clenched his fist when he realized how right Yasmeena was. He had known it, of course. But he did not want to think about it. This was not like him. He was not thinking clearly. Not thinking far enough ahead. The unprotected sex. Committing to being this woman's business partner. Her chef! Was he insane? Was he seriously losing his mind? There was a limit to jumping into things without considering the consequences, was there not? And had he finally crossed that limit? Goddamn it. *Goddamn it!*

"So you understand," Yasmeena said.

Kabeer smiled, his lips so tight they looked white with constriction. "Yes."

"And so you also understand that you will need to

be publicly linked with another woman so that the press cannot even speculate that you are involved with Jenny. I do not care who the other woman is, but it would be useful if it were someone photogenic and famous. That shouldn't be a problem, should it?"

Kabeer looked at her as a chill ran up his spine. But he held his poker face. He could not let Yasmeena know what he was feeling. Allah, he couldn't let *himself* admit what he was feeling!

Yasmeena smiled now. "A model, actress, heiress, . . . whatever," she said, leaning back in her chair and looking right at Kabeer with a strange pointedness, like she was testing him, watching his reaction to this. "You can even do your thing of being seen with three different women in a week. But it will be crucial that you are *always* with another woman—we cannot have you single and working closely with Jenny for even a *day*. The rumors would start instantly, and it would change the story in a way that could hurt us."

Kabeer nodded slowly as he stood up. His legs felt weak even as every muscle in his body tensed up. He wanted to punch something, smash something, *destroy* something. But he had learned how to control himself, and he turned away from his sister and headed for the door. This was fine. He could work through this. He was just turned around right now, knocked off balance by this woman Jenny, taken by surprise by the attraction he felt when he was close to her, the feeling he got when he looked into those brown eyes, the electricity that ripped through his body when he touched her curves.

It will pass, he told himself as he reached for the door. Yasmeena is just trying to get under my skin, trying to get me to back off from getting involved with this restaurant. That is all it is.

But is that all, he wondered as he stopped before walking out. There was certainly the feeling that Yasmeena had been testing him when she talked about him not getting romantically involved with Jenny, about publicly seeing other women so the press would pick it up. What was his sister up to? Was she trying to figure out if he actually felt something for this American woman? If it was more than sex, more than a physical dalliance, more than a frivolous romp? But why would Yasmeena care so much? So what if he wanted something more with Jenny, if he actually began to care about her? Yes, there would be complications with the public relations, but that could be worked out, couldn't it? Yasmeena would know that.

So is there some other reason why Yasmeena does not want me and Jenny to get involved. There is something that concerns her about me and Jenny. What? And why?

"I am not finished, Kabeer," Yasmeena said now.

Kabeer was startled, wondering how long he had been standing there by the door. But now it occurred to him that it had only been a couple of seconds, and he cleared his mind and sighed. "What now, Yasmeena? You want a chaperone with me and Jenny at all times?"

"No, Kabeer. No. There is something else." Her voice was soft, almost sad.

Kabeer turned now, eyebrows raised. "Yes. Go on."

"Come, sit, brother," Yasmeena said as she folded her arms across her chest, the satin red tunic throwing off flashes of light as it crinkled under the pressure. She glanced down at herself, and then up at Kabeer, a deep, meaningful look in her eyes. "Please," she said quietly.

Kabeer took a step towards his sister, frowning as an inexplicable sense of dread entered him from the expression on his sister's face, the way her voice shook, that faraway look in her eyes as she glanced back at that old photo. "What in Allah's name is going on? If this is about separating me from Jenny, that is ridiculous. I barely know the woman, and I could not care—"

"Father is dead, Kabeer," Yasmeena said suddenly, trying to force a smile as the words caught in her throat. She held the plastic smile as a tear gathered at the corner of her left eye. She blinked now, and the tear slowly rolled down her cheek. "He passed two hours ago, in comfort, on his own terms. In his home. Our home. I asked that no one inform you. I wanted to tell you myself. He asked me to tell you myself."

Kabeer shivered involuntarily. It felt like all the blood had suddenly drained from his body. He looked at his sister. She was composed now, and instead of grief, he suddenly felt anger.

"You spoke to him? You knew this was happening? And I am not told of it? I am the goddamn *last* to know?! How dare you? How *dare* you?!"

Kabeer pushed back in his seat, the heavy chair screeching back from the table. He staggered to his feet now, for once truly afraid of the energy that raged through his body. He stormed to the far end of the sprawling, wood-paneled office, stopping at a floor-to-ceiling bookshelf filled with leather-bound volumes. He clenched his fists, ground his teeth, shut his eyes so tight it made him dizzy. He resisted the urge to strike at the wood, and he took several deep breaths before finally resting his head against the rows of books. Now the grief rushed in, and Kabeer swallowed hard as he allowed himself one deep, private sob that he could not contain.

"Why?" he said. "Why did he not tell me? Why did he not speak to me? Why you and not me, Yasmeena? For him it has always been you and not me, has it not? Is that why?"

Yasmeena snorted, her eyes going wide, and for a moment she looked like that child again, that serious older sister that only Kabeer could make squeal with laughter in those happy days that seemed like another life. She smiled now, disbelief in her eyes as she looked up at her brother.

"Oh, Kabeer," she whispered. "You do not see it,

do you? Of course you do not. For Father, there was no you and me, no him and her. It was always about duty, responsibly, and service. Service to his nation, his people, his God. Our nation, our people, our God."

Kabeer paced the room now, trying to control the cacophony of thoughts, the maze of emotions. He stopped and looked up now, almost quizzical. "But this is how you tell me, Yasmeena? This is how you tell me our father is dead? You call a business meeting? It is all business to you?"

Yasmeena sighed now, glancing at that old photograph one more time. "Perhaps. But this is how Father wanted it done. He said he wanted it to be unexpected. Shocking. He said it would rouse you from your sleep."

Kabeer blinked and shook his head like a dog at the beach. "Are you mad, Yasmeena? Was my father mad as well? Rouse me? *Rouse* me?! Well, I am awake now, by Allah! What does he want from me?"

Yasmeena looked at him without expression. "You know what he wants from you. And he knows that you are too stubborn to ever listen to reason, to listen to argument, even to obey his direct command." Now she shrugged. "So Father did what he thought would shock you into action. He wanted to short-circuit your brain, forcing you to bypass your cold intelligence, leaving you with nothing but your instincts, your feelings, your gut, your *heart* to follow. Father said that was the only way a man can get in touch with his deepest purpose in life, what he was born to do, the man he was born to be. Do you see, Kabeer?"

Kabeer stood there in the middle of the room as the walls closed in on him. The rug beneath his feet started to spin. The very ceiling cracked down the middle. He looked up and he could see into heaven, he thought, and there was his father, that mischief in his eyes, that smile on his lips. Kabeer's mother was beside him, as were the spirits of his ancestors, and all of them were looking down at him, waiting for him to make his choice.

Now Yasmeena walked up to her brother, touching him on the arm, now touching his face as she looked into his eyes with a warmth Kabeer had not seen in her for a long time.

"He yearned to speak with you one last time, Kabeer," she whispered.

"Why did he not?" Kabeer managed to say.

"Because he wanted you to remember the last thing he said to you."

"What was that?" Kabeer said, frowning as he tried to replay that last meeting with his father.

"I do not know, Kabeer. I was not there. And Father did not tell me."

Kabeer sighed and turned around, nodding and shaking his head all at once as he walked to the window and stared out across downtown Chicago. The bustling city suddenly looked cold and lifeless to him, and he felt a strange, wistful longing for the heat of the Bukhaara sun, the cool dry air of the desert evenings, the sweet smell of cinnamon tea, the distant sounds of Arabian drumbeats. And as those images flooded his mind, a clarity came along with it, calming his soul, stilling his thoughts, giving him the strangest of peace.

Ya Allah, he thought as he watched the yellow taxis on the street below transform into majestic camels, the paved city streets now looking like the packed sand of the roads through the deserts, the fountain on Webster Street turning into the great oasis of Bukhaara. What was it Father said to me?

Then it came back to him, the last words he heard from his Father:

Sometimes it is just when you think you are escaping your destiny that you are in fact running towards it.

And now it all came to Kabeer in a flash, and as he stormed out of that dark, wood-paneled office, he knew there was no escaping destiny. Not for him. And not for her.

Not for her.

15

"**W**hat do you mean you will not see me? By God, you are going to see me if I have to—"

"I didn't say I won't see you, Kabeer. I said I *can't* see you. Not right now. I've got a million things to do. I've got a meeting to negotiate the lease for the space. Then I'm talking with the interior designers and architects. I haven't even *started* talking supplier contracts with the food vendors. And all of this happens before I can even begin to think about staffing and hiring. I'm going insane right now—good insane, but insane. Just give me some space, all right?"

"*Space*? Jenny, it has been *one month* and this is the first time you've even answered my call! I would have stormed into your apartment weeks ago, but I have been in Bukhaara attending to a personal family matter. Besides, I do not storm into the apartments of my women without—"

"Your *women*, Kabeer? Plural?" Jenny almost spat the words out, and the moment she said it she knew she had screwed up. She had shown her hand. Shown him that she gave a shit. That it mattered. That maybe *he* mattered.

She moved the phone away from her ear and mouthed out an expletive and almost stomped her foot, she was so damned angry with herself. This could *not* be happening to her right now. She could *not* be falling for someone at the exact time she needed her wits about her.

Calm down, she told herself, just like she had been telling herself for three weeks now. One out-of-character escapade doesn't mean you're falling for him. Lust is not the same as love, even though it's easily confused in the moment. You're smarter than this, Jenny. Wiser, more experienced, *stronger*. You're staring at the chance of a lifetime with this financing. Don't screw it up for some billionaire playboy just because he made you come a few times.

Oh, but how I came, she remembered—not like she had ever forgotten! You don't forget passion like that. If anything, the wonderful chaos of the past few weeks—signing the offer sheet, seeing the money come through, walking through that beautiful space off Michigan Avenue with the knowledge that it would soon be hers . . . yes, the madness of the past three weeks had only *heightened* the memory of that intense hour with Kabeer, in the open air on that yacht, beneath the cloudless sky, the burning sun . . . oh, God, that *was* real, wasn't it?

"Jenny?" came his voice over the phone. "Are you still there, little Jenny?"

Jenny shook herself out of it and cleared her throat, thinking of what Yasmeena had told her. This was business now. All business. "Kabeer, don't call me that. We're going to be working together, and so—"

"What, so you are Ms. Jones to me now?" He paused now, his voice low when he spoke again. "And was that Ms. Jones's lips I kissed three weeks ago? Was it Ms. Jones who shivered and moaned in my arms as I pulled down her wet panties and—"

"*Stop it!*" Jenny screamed. "That was *one* time! The *only* time. You said so yourself—once I signed the contract, it's all business."

"Actually I never said that," Kabeer replied. "I said that it was one-hundred percent personal until you signed the contract. I did not say anything else."

"Well, I told you what Yasmeena said, Kabeer. And she's right—"

"What did Yasmeena say? When? Has she spoken to you recently?"

Jenny hesitated. Then she took a deep breath and answered. "Yasmeena and I have spoken several times over the past three weeks. She's been very involved in putting me in touch with the right people as I get things organized. She really knows how to—"

"Not that, Jenny," Kabeer snapped, his anger coming through clearly, as if he had lost control for a second. He went quiet immediately, and Jenny heard him breathe like he was trying to control himself. "I am sorry," he said finally. "But you know what I meant, Jenny. Did my sister say anything about me? About us? Do not lie to me, Jenny."

She almost snapped back at him, almost reminded him that there was no "us!" But she couldn't help feel a tingling warmth that threatened to melt her as she listened to Kabeer talk, listened to him speak about them like there could be something there, like there already *was* something there! Still, she held back as she considered what to say next, and of course there was nothing to think about. She didn't do bullshit. Lying or skirting around the truth was too much overhead. So she sighed and just told him.

"Yes, Kabeer. Yasmeena told me everything. She made it clear that I could not be romantically involved with you if I wanted this restaurant to succeed." She paused, her breath catching as she spoke her next words carefully, dispassionately, like she had practiced ever since Yasmeena had explained in no uncertain terms what it would mean if she and Kabeer even looked like they were together. "Yasmeena explained everything, and she's absolutely right. I agree with her. What happened on the boat—that was . . . fun. Yes, it was fun. But that's all it was. Fun. So let's just stick with the story—which is a *true* story, by the way."

"The true story . . ." Kabeer said, and Jenny could almost hear him grind his teeth over the phone.

"Yes," Jenny said, struggling to keep her voice steady. "That our relationship is professional and nothing more, and you'll be up to your usual . . . um . . . your usual . . . I mean, what you usually . . ."

She couldn't finish the sentence, because something inside wouldn't let the words come out. There was a silence now, a silence so heavy that it felt like it might crush her.

Finally he spoke.

"OK, Jenny," Kabeer said, his voice deafeningly calm now, like a switch had flipped in him, a light had gone out. "Sorry. I mean Ms. Jones."

"Oh, come on, Kabeer. You don't have to—"

"Let me know when you are ready to start talking business. Until then, good luck and goodbye. I have other matters to attend to." He hung up without waiting for a reply.

Jenny stared at the phone as the most sickening feeling washed over her. She was nauseas, sick to her

stomach, dizzy and lightheaded. She glanced in despair at the papers scattered all over her desk, looked
at the "Congratulations!" cards from her best friends
and classmates, the smiley faces she had drawn on
the hundreds of post-it notes that dotted her com-
puter monitor . . . yes, she looked at all the remind-
ers of happiness, success, and optimism; and then
she turned away and forced a smile as she got back
to work.

What choice did she have? She couldn't choose a
"maybe-perhaps-possibly" romance with a man she
barely knew, a man who was getting calls and messages from models and movie stars, a man who could
and would walk away if he got bored with plain old
Jenny Jones, a man who seemed American enough at
times but very much not American at other times, a
man who had this whole side of him which she knew
nothing about!

Yes, what did she know about Bukhaara, about
Sheikhs and rulers, about their religion, their poli-
tics, their language, their land, their people? Nothing.

So she knew almost nothing about Kabeer, and so
of *course* she was making the right choice by honestly
and truly accepting the conditions Yasmeena had set
forth in how she should conduct her business, how
she should conduct herself. The relationship with Kabeer stays professional, Jenny, or else you risk losing
everything, you risk being left with nothing. Nothing
except a memory of what might have been.

Now Jenny looked down at herself and touched her stomach, patting the cute bulge of her belly as she sighed for a reason she did not want to acknowledge. She had taken the morning-after pill following the boat trip, but she couldn't deny that for some strange reason she had hesitated a long time before doing it. Perhaps too long? No, she was fine. She couldn't be pregnant. It would take a miracle. An act of God. No need to think about it.

"Jump in, right, Grandma?" she said out loudly to the empty room, patting her belly again as she pushed all her thoughts aside and tried desperately to focus on her work. "Jump in."

16

"**D**ubai?"

"Dubai."

It had been over a month since their father's death, and things seemed to have settled down, so Yasmeena looked at her brother with some apprehension as she put her bag down on the table of her office. Kabeer had been waiting for her to arrive, and it looked like he had been in the office a while.

"Dubai," Yasmeena said again, clearing her throat as she took her seat and looked into her brother's eyes to see if he was sober. "In the United Arab Emirates?

That Dubai? You want the first location of Jenny's restaurant business to be in Dubai? Not Chicago. Not New York. Not Paris. Not London. Dubai."

Kabeer nodded. "I think you have got it, Yasmeena. Dubai. Correct."

Yasmeena tried to keep her breathing calm even though her heart was pounding. In a way she was not too surprised. She and Kabeer had just returned from almost three weeks in Bukhaara, and Yasmeena had proudly watched her brother perform the funeral rites for their father, the old Sheikh. Indeed, Kabeer had made no argument when told by his father's council of advisors about the details of the funeral, the ceremonies and speeches that would need to be given, the prayer calls and scheduled visits to the great mosques of Bukhaara that would have to be conducted. More importantly, Kabeer had made no fuss or protest when the council informed him that in six months, after the mourning period had passed, he would ascend to be Sheikh of Bukhaara.

The Sheikh of Bukhaara.

Yasmeena had almost cried with joy as she watched her brother step out through the dark purple curtain on the massive funeral stage erected in the center of Bukhaara's capital. It was a somber occasion, and so the thousands who thronged the narrow streets were relatively quiet as Kabeer emerged, dressed in the royal robes, purple, blue, and red silk intertwined with black satin, green velvet. On his head he wore one of the royal turbans handed down through the generations of Bukhaara's Sheikhs—Kabeer and Yasmeena's ancestors, their bloodline, their family.

The turban was trimmed with gold that was hand-embroidered by their great-grandmothers, studded with diamonds, rubies, and emeralds that were over a hundred years old. It certainly looked like a crown fit for the greatest of kings. But Yasmeena knew it was not the royal crown itself. No, because although Kabeer was already Sheikh simply by virtue of his line, the ascendancy ceremony would not occur for another six months, not until the mourning period for the old Sheikh had passed.

And a lot could happen in six months.

Like this sudden plan about Dubai. It has come out of nowhere, Yasmeena thought. And although she was pleased that Kabeer seemed to want to return to the Middle-East—indeed, Dubai was less than an hour's flight from Bukhaara—she needed to be certain about his motives.

"Kabeer," she said quietly. "We have only just returned from burying our father. We are still grieving. Perhaps this is not the time to make sudden decisions."

"It is not sudden. I have been considering it for the past three weeks. I took several day-trips to Dubai while we were in Bukhaara. I already have a space picked out."

Yasmeena did a double take. "You left Bukhaara during the funeral period? I did not know of it."

Kabeer smiled, his eyes bright and focused, his jaw set. "Nobody knew of it. I have a pilot's license, remember?"

Yasmeena sighed and nodded. "Kabeer," she said quietly, intently, almost a plea in her voice. "You are the Sheikh of Bukhaara now. You realize that, do you not?"

Kabeer held her gaze. No head movement. Not even a blink. "Not until the ascendancy ceremony. But yes, I do realize I will be Sheikh. That I am Sheikh. I have always known the day would come, Yasmeena. I ran from it as long as I could, but I know my time is coming."

Yasmeena tried to hide her joy. "Then why are you wasting your time and energy on this restaurant business! You should be preparing to lead your people! Speaking with the council of advisors on a regular basis! Traveling your land, meeting your people, getting to know them once again! Let me run our businesses, like I have always done! You have a nation to run, brother! A people to lead! Drop this Dubai nonsense! And this chef nonsense! We cannot have the Sheikh of Bukhaara cooking in a restaurant in Dubai! Our people would be the laughing stock of the Middle East! As it is there is much work to do on your image, Kabeer. As it is there is a lot of damage to be undone, ya Allah! Do not make it worse!"

But Kabeer stayed silent, and now it was Yasmeena's turn to feel a strange thought enter her being as she looked at her brother, looked into his eyes. She took a breath, choosing her words carefully. Then she spoke, hoping she could play this right, test her brother the way she wanted to test him.

"Oh, God, Kabeer. This is not about that woman, is it? It cannot be about her, can it? Jenny Jones? This American who . . . who spread for you the first damned chance she—"

"*Don't!*" Kabeer shouted, *slamming* his palms down on the cold wood table with such force that Yasmeena jerked backwards, almost hitting the padded wall behind her chair. "Don't," Kabeer said again, pointing at his sister, his face flush with color as he tried to calm himself down.

Yasmeena took several deep breaths before speaking. "But . . . but Kabeer . . . it has been weeks since you have even seen her! You yourself said that you barely know her. And now you want to drag her to the Middle-East so you can . . . so you can . . . so you can what? It does not make any sense, Kabeer! It doesn't even—"

"She's pregnant," Kabeer blurted out now. "Yasmeena, she is pregnant. With my child. That is what makes sense of everything. Jenny is going to have my baby. That is the only thing that you need to understand. You understand, do you not? Jenny Jones is carrying the child of the Sheikh of Bukhaara. A royal child."

17

Dubai.

The United Arab Emirates.

Dubai.

If the past three weeks had been chaos and madness, what was happening now didn't have a name. Ridiculousness? Insanity? Ridiculous insanity?

Which part is ridiculous, Jenny, she had asked herself as she packed her bags and made sure all the stoves were off in her cozy little apartment kitchen. Yes, which part is ridiculous? The part where a private courier in a purple uniform shows up with a letter and a set of documents—the letter informing you that Bukhaara Capital has made the unilateral decision (that means they just do it without asking, Jenny discovered . . .) that the first location of Global Kitchen (*her* restaurant, *her* idea, *her* business, by the way . . .) will be in Dubai, a city in the United Arab Emirates? How about the part where you calmly read the rest of the documents, which include an amended agreement (amended without asking, without negotiating . . .) that allows you to back out of the contract, to walk away from the business. You would be paid back the entire personal investment, as well as a lumpsum payout for the work already put in, as well as the rights to the business plan.

In other words Jenny was being told that she needed to move to Dubai, or else she'd be moved out . . . out of her own company! Was this a test? A test to see how far they could push her? A test to see how badly she wanted this? Still, Bukhaara Capital was the majority owner, and their "boilerplate" standard agreement gave them almost complete (unilateral . . .) authority over the business and its personnel. Complete authority over Jenny too, it seemed.

So was that ridiculous? Or was it ridiculous that while the dark-skinned courier stood there like a mute footman from the horror-movie version of Cinderella, Jenny thought for about three minutes, and then signed the new agreement and began packing.

She didn't bother to call Bukhaara Capital. By now

she understood how things worked with this company, with this family. Yasmeena and Kabeer were in charge. She couldn't be sure whose idea this was, or why this was happening, but she didn't want to think about it. In a strange way she was already prepared—mentally prepared, that is—for something like this.

Perhaps it was because over the past few weeks she had been so absorbed in thinking about her business in real, concrete, this-is-happening terms, about "First Chicago, then the world!" as she expanded to other countries. Yes, perhaps because she already knew that Global Kitchen would eventually have locations on every continent—certainly in the Middle-East, perhaps beginning with Dubai anyway—it didn't seem like a *totally* insane idea to start outside the United States.

But it wasn't just that, and she knew it. It was him. Sheikh Kabeer Bukhaara. Her billionaire-celebrity-chef. He was behind this—she sensed it the moment that gaudily dressed courier buzzed her apartment from downstairs. What the hell was Kabeer doing? Certainly Jenny had expected that he wouldn't simply take no for an answer, that she'd constantly need to be on her guard, pushing him back as they struggled to find a working relationship after the way things had started between them. But she was prepared for that—or at least that's what she told herself.

But Dubai . . . oh, God, in a way it's as exciting and

thrilling as it is ridiculous and insane, isn't it? But Kabeer, what are you thinking? What do you think is going to happen? Do you want to get me on your turf, in the Middle-East, far out of my comfort zone? Is that your game? You think I'll fall into your arms because we're in some strange foreign land? You think it'll be that easy to get me to sell out my business, my goals, my goddamn *dreams* for some good sex?

But it wasn't just "good sex," she thought as she zipped up that bag and checked herself in the mirror. She touched her face, her cheeks, her chin. She straightened her hair, her blue blouse, her black jeans. Then she touched her belly again, like she had been doing almost unconsciously a lot this past month, this past month which had been so busy, so hectic, so chaotic that she had missed meals, missed personal appointments, missed her . . . missed her . . . wait, what was the date . . . what was the damned date . . . ohgod . . . .ohgod . . . ohgod . . . *ohmygod*!

And now Jenny *ran* to the bathroom, her hand over her mouth as she felt the sickness rise in her like a panic, and now it was real panic that tore through her as she threw up in the sink, and suddenly she was crying, sobbing, shaking . . . and now she was laughing, giggling, drooling . . . and all of it spun around and around until she just collapsed on the soft blue bathroom rug and broke down into all of it—laughter and tears, shaking and coughing, gurgling and whimpering, the sounds of a madwoman, the sounds of an animal, the sounds of . . . of . . . a child.

A child.

A royal child.

18

"**G**lobe. That's the name. Not Global Kitchen, but Globe. One word. Globe," Jenny said. It wasn't a question, and it certainly wasn't a suggestion. It was a statement, pure and simple. Spoken with authority.

Jenny was seated at a round table at the prime spot in her still-being-constructed restaurant interior, the frosted glass windows overlooking the deep blue Gulf of Oman. Dubai was a port city, Jenny had discovered as she flew in and saw the ocean meet the desert, the shining spires of Dubai's new city looking like an alien landscape from the air. Her driver had taken her through the old city on the way to her hotel, and

Jenny had been transfixed by the white sandstone houses nestled together along the narrow, cobblestone streets, the street vendors calling out in Arabic as they sold everything from fresh dates to ancient crystals of desert glass picked from the expanses of pure white sand that enveloped the region.

Kabeer had already selected a space, Jenny was informed, and although she wasn't sure if she wanted to hate it or not, once she saw it she had to admit that it was something she herself would have chosen.

The space was circular, just like the space Jenny had wanted in Chicago. It was at the ground level facing the patio of the Burj Khalifa atrium. The Burj Khalifa, Jenny discovered, was the tallest building in the world, and it drew visitors from all over the globe, visitors who would stand in line for three hours just to get to the top and take in the view. Then they would come down, ravenous and ready to spend money. And "Globe" would be right there.

Not yet, though. There was a lot of work to be done. Even as Jenny had prepared for Yasmeena's visit, contractors were working on an etched stone wall towards the west side, furniture people were polishing the beautiful antique wooden benches she had placed near the front in the waiting area, the sounds of top-of-the-line stainless-steel appliances being moved into place were ringing out from the large open kitchen.

Yasmeena Bukhaara had arrived alone, nodding at Jenny and then sitting across from her at the round table. And now here they were.

"Globe," Jenny said again. "It works."

Yasmeena's eyes narrowed, and Jenny could see her perusing a mental checklist. But Jenny wasn't worried. This was the name, and she wasn't going to back down if Yasmeena hated it. She had compromised enough. This was her baby now, and a mother always gets to name her child, doesn't she?

"Globe," Yasmeena repeated. A long pause. Then "Globe," again, like she was going into a trance. Slowly she began to nod, a straight smile finally emerging on her thin lips. "Globe. One word. It's tight, elegant, and evocative. Fits the elite image we're trying to portray. Sounds intriguing enough for people to look us up and see what kind of cuisine we serve." She nodded again. "And it's broad enough to travel well as the name of an international chain." She looked around the room. "Oh, and it fits perfectly with the circular shape of the space!" Now the smile was full, and she glanced at the craftsmen working on the stone and wood and nodded. "I like it," she finally said. "It is coming together. I like it."

Jenny grinned, allowing herself to feel some relief. "Do you love it?"

Yasmeena's tight smile opened up and she actually showed a flash of teeth, but she didn't reward

Jenny with anything more. Soon enough her surly expression was back, and she glanced around with that birdlike intensity.

"It is shaping up well, but there is still a long way to go before we can even get a few publicity shots of the interior. We need to launch in the winter, Jenny. Winter is peak season in Dubai, because the temperatures are tolerable in the day and cool at night. If we have a big opening that carries through the tourist and holiday season, it could give us the momentum we need to have a solid first year. And if it goes well, perhaps we can think about a second location a year, maybe eighteen months, from now."

Jenny blinked as her breath caught. A second location in a year? The financing so far had strictly been for the first location, so to hear Yasmeena even mention the possibility of a second location so soon . . . well, it meant that surly Ms. Bukhaara was feeling optimistic!

Not that her pallid demeanor let on she was feeling anything, let alone unbridled optimism. Another quick look around, a few specific questions about timing, a comment about having a contact with someone at the Dubai Department of Health, and then she was on her feet and headed for the door.

"I haven't even had the food samples brought out yet," Jenny said in surprise, looking up at the tall, pencil-thin woman. Jenny caught herself before she asked if Kabeer would be joining or not. "Don't you want to at least *see* what the dishes look like?"

"Food's not my thing," Yasmeena said with a shrug that was more a "deal-with-it" shrug than an apologetic one. "Unless it is something that our head chef has cooked. How is my brother's cooking, anyway? Can the man even boil an egg?"

Jenny's heart jumped but she didn't even blink. She had called Kabeer when she arrived in Dubai, but Kabeer had said he was staying in Bukhaara, immersing himself in the world of culinary arts, learning the fundamentals, getting it "under his skin." It was something he needed to do alone, he told her.

"It is my process," he had said. "Every time I decide to dedicate myself to learning a new skill, I immerse myself in it completely for a period of absolute focus. I study every resource available. I watch the masters at work. I practice and experiment on my own. I pay for exclusive lessons if I need them. But I need to do it alone so I can feel free to fail, make a mess of things. It is my process, and when I am done I will be ready to be a head chef. I promise you that. I'll have the basics down so damn right, that I will soak in whatever new things you have to teach me. Then I shall be all yours, Jenny."

Jenny had been heartened to hear his voice sound casual and friendly, even excited. That coldness was no longer there. Of course, that warmth, that passion, that heat was no longer there either, but that was for the best, wasn't it? Wasn't it?

So "Immerse yourself, Chef," is what she said, sounding as casual and friendly as she could in return. "The timing works out, actually, because the kitchen should be ready to go by then. We can get right down to work, and we'll have a solid three months before launch to get ready. So do what you need to, and I'll see you in three weeks!"

It had felt good, that casual conversation with Kabeer, and Jenny had put down the phone feeling some confidence that they would in fact be able to work together just fine. So they had slept together. Big deal! She was an adult American woman! So she slept with a man that she'd now be working with! Happens all the time in America. Everywhere else in the world too! Successful women deal with shit like that!

As for the pregnancy . . . well, successful women deal with shit like that too! And there was *plenty* of time to deal with that once the restaurant was up and running and she was on her way. Yes. Plenty of time. You're fine. You're good. Everything's OK. Breathe. Inhale. Suppress. Repress. Bury and forget. Whew. Done. So easy! Whoop-dee-doo! All gone!

Still, that simple phone interaction had relieved a lot of tension. It had felt good, good enough that she was more-or-less able to handle it like a grown-up when she saw his name in the gossip feeds, linked with a South American swimsuit model. ("Really, Kabeer?" was the only comment she allowed herself to make—in private, of course.)

She had resisted the urge to check out a picture of the woman—the blurb of "swimsuit model" evoked a clear enough image. But two days after seeing the headline, Jenny reminded herself that the press Kabeer got would ultimately play into the overall marketing story for the restaurant, and so it was actually her business to see what this woman looked like!

So she had pulled up a picture of the woman— Selena Rai, age twenty-three—on her phone while supervising the installation of a stainless-steel bar near the waiting area of the restaurant.

Jenny had been distracted as the picture downloaded, and when she glanced back at her phone and finally saw what this Selena woman (girl, really...) looked like, she almost fell off her high chair.

Because the woman was not an emaciated, hollowed out, ghost of a woman—the sort Jenny had pegged as Kabeer's type. No, this woman had curves—*serious* curves! Wide, well-rounded hips. Healthy breasts that looked large and natural. Thick thighs that looked like they shuddered when she walked. And a booty that Jenny knew would show some cellulite if it hadn't been Photoshopped to unnatural perfection. Granted, she was brown-skinned and tanned, with curly dark hair and full lips. She was also a bit(!)

younger. But Jenny couldn't help but think, as she scrolled through more pictures until she found a candid street-shot taken from a distance, that this woman sorta kinda looked like . . .

"No," she had told herself, quickly deleting the history in her phone browser and then putting the phone away. "Do not even start. You've made your choice, and it's the right choice. Don't lose your nerve."

Don't lose your nerve, Jenny told herself now as she watched Yasmeena wait for an answer. You can answer Yasmeena's simple question about Kabeer's cooking without revealing how messed up your feelings are about this, without revealing how you're somehow handling the fact that you're pregnant with his child while he is out there with some Brazilian swimsuit model, doing God-knows-what with her! Yes, she hadn't told him yet—which was unfair in a way. But how could she? She didn't know how he'd react! What if he didn't want it. Didn't want *her* . . . now that she was . . .

Oh God, she thought as she forced a surprisingly convincing smile and nodded at Yasmeena. Don't cry. You cannot cry. It will all work out. You're doing the right thing by keeping your focus on your goal, your work, your dream. Don't blow it by losing your shit—at least not here, not now, not with this woman!

"Kabeer's in Bukhaara," Jenny said pleasantly, that smile really hurting her face as she held it. "So no, I made the samples."

"Kabeer has returned to Bukhaara? When did he leave?" Yasmeena said with a quizzical frown.

Now Jenny frowned. "Leave from where? The U.S.?"

"Dubai, of course. He was here these past few weeks, was he not? Here with you?"

"No," Jenny said, blinking rapidly as she felt those thoughts and emotions banging at the doors in her head, like they were going to burst through and demand answers, demand action, demand resolution. Oh, God, was it a mistake not to tell him? Shouldn't he know? Wouldn't he be happy? It was more than sex, wasn't it? He'll be happy, won't he? He's not really sleeping with that Brazilian nymph, is he? He's in love with me, isn't he?

In love with me? Are *you* in love with *him*?! A man you've known for less than two months, whom you've spent a couple of days with, slept with just once, and whose child you are now carrying . . . in *secret*? How does love fit into it? How *can* love fit into it?!

And now she felt herself choking on her own emotion, gagging on her own thoughts, dizzy from her own paranoia. And suddenly she felt a bony arm on her shoulder, and it was Yasmeena who had come around to her side of the table, and Jenny looked into her gray eyes like it was a dream again, that surreal dream where she was a part of something, a part of this family . . . just like she was carrying a child of this family within her womb.

"You know," Yasmeena was saying as Jenny tried to

blink away the tears before realizing that she wasn't crying at all, that somehow she had maintained her composure while everything came apart inside her. So then why the hell was Yasmeena sitting by her, arm around Jenny, her tone conveying a warmth that seemed so unusual for this woman, so unexpected that Jenny told herself again that it was just a dream and perhaps she had been working too hard and sleeping too little and ohgod maybe the hormone things have started already and—

"You know," Yasmeena said. "In that very first meeting I realized Kabeer saw something in you, that he felt something for you. In the past ten years, do you know how many women Kabeer has brought into my presence, into his father's presence?"

Jenny just shook her head. She might look composed, but she knew she couldn't trust herself to say even one goddamn word right now.

"One," Yasmeena said. "Just one, Jenny. Just you, Jenny. I know you did not realize it at the time, and the funny thing is, I do not think Kabeer realized it either! He was just going with his instincts, trusting his gut without really thinking it through explicitly." Now she took a breath. "But I know my brother better than anyone. And his instincts have always been dead right, spot on, eerily prophetic. So when I realized that this woman who he was carrying up the stairway to our boat was the same woman whose business proposal and references impressed me, I knew I had to invest in your idea, bring you into the company." Yasmeena touched Jenny's arm in a strange, sisterly way. "I mean, Bukhaara Capital would have eventually invested in Globe anyway, but I did it right then because I wanted to . . . to bring you into the family myself. Yes, I wanted to bring you into the family myself, just in case my brother . . ." She sighed now, looked away for a moment like she was searching for the right words, and then turned back to Jenny. "What I'm trying to say is that alongside these otherworldly instincts that Kabeer possesses, there is also a perverse stubbornness in him, and sometimes he . . . how to put it . . . sometimes he purposely turns away from the direction his instincts are pointing. But it never lasts. He turned away from the Sheikhood for so long, but now he seems ready to turn back to it, to his country, his people, his God. And although I was not sure if he would make it through all the obstacles I set for him . . ."

"Obstacles to what?" Jenny asked, speaking like she was in a trance.

Yasmeena smiled, looking down for a moment before holding Jenny's gaze and flashing an almost apologetic smile. "Obstacles to you, Jenny. Obstacles to claiming you! Many things have come too easy for Kabeer, especially women. I wanted him to understand what it means to want someone badly enough that you will oppose your family, disregard your business, even go against your tradition and culture to be with her." Yasmeena laughed now. "I am a clear and logical person, but even I know that logic and reason have no place in matters of the heart. In matters of love. And so, although my logical brain told me it will be a publicity nightmare for your restaurant, I felt nothing but pure joy when Kabeer told me!"

"Told you what?" Jenny said from that trance.

"The news, of course!" Yasmeena said. "I did not reach out to you earlier because Kabeer told me not to, that he wanted it to stay private for now, at least until the Dubai location was launched. But I see no reason to not congratulate you right now, now that you have chosen to come to Dubai, to the Middle-East, to have his child in Bukhaara itself!"

"Wait, what?" was all Jenny could say before she almost knocked over the round table as she ran for the bathroom, not sure if it was morning sickness or afternoon madness that was turning her inside out, upside down, twisted around.

19

Kabeer looked at himself in the mirror of the Presidential Suite at the Jumeirah Grand Hotel in Dubai. He touched his face, ran his hands along the stubble that was not as manicured as he would like. His hair was longer too, and there were bags under his normally sharp eyes from the sleepless nights, the harrowing days.

He still could not believe he had lied to Yasmeena about Jenny being pregnant. But what was more unbelievable was his sister's reaction! Ya, Allah, she had shouted with *joy*! Has the world gone mad? I tell Yasmeena that this middle-class American woman, this woman that my sister called a whore to her face, to *my* face . . . yes, I tell Yasmeena that this woman who apparently is "not photogenic enough" to be seen with me is carrying my child, the first of the next generation of Bukhaara's royal family, and Yasmeena is *happy*?!

Kabeer was certain she would fly into a rage, perhaps even faint. She would curse him, curse her, curse the child even! She would say the child should never be born because it would bring disgrace on the house of Bukhaara, scandal to our people! That is what Kabeer expected from his sister.

And that is what Kabeer wanted from his sister.

Yes, he wanted Yasmeena to go down that same old path, asking him with fury if this is how a Sheikh conducts himself, spreading his royal seed amongst women he barely knows, brash American women with no understanding of Bukhaara, its people and culture. Yasmeena would say this was unworthy of a Sheikh, that *he* was unworthy of being Sheikh.

And Kabeer would agree.

"You are correct, dear sister," he would say to Yasmeena as he tried to contain a smile of victory. "I am not worthy of being a leader. I would only bring scandal to our people, shame to our family, cast a shadow on our nation. It must be you, dear Yasmeena. You must return to Bukhaara and take up the mantle of Sheikha. The people will remember you, and they will accept you."

But Kabeer never got a chance to play out that game, because Yasmeena broke the rules! And her joy was real, her happiness true, her look of delight so clear that she seemed like a child herself in that moment as she hugged me. *Hugged* me! Allah, Yasmeena has not hugged me in years!

Now he stared at his reflection in the mirror once again. He looked into his own green eyes that so often helped him get what he wanted, when he wanted, how he wanted. And then he thought of his sister, of what she had said to him after he had told her—after he had *lied* to her—about Jenny being pregnant with his child.

"Oh, Kabeer," Yasmeena had said as she kissed him on either cheek. "Ya, Allah. God is great. It may not be according to tradition in so many ways, and there will be many who will shake their heads when the news spreads, but I do not care. I knew this woman was special from that first day, Kabeer."

"You called her a whore on that first day, Yasmeena," Kabeer had said, flabbergasted at his sister's *completely* unexpected reaction.

"I wanted to see your reaction, Kabeer! I have my instincts too, you know! We are the same blood. We come from the same line. I saw something in the two of you that day, and that side of me came out to test you, to test both of you. It was not fully conscious, perhaps not fully calculated—at least not at first."

"What do you mean 'not at first,' Yasmeena?"

Yasmeena shook her head as if to clear it, her eyes still wide like a child's. "The moment you told me you wanted to be the celebrity chef at Jenny's restaurant, I knew I was right. I knew that even though you had not reasoned it out, your instincts were leading you, telling you to stay by her side, no matter what the consequences! That is all that is required for true love, my mother used to say! A natural, spontaneous willingness to do even the most silly, ridiculous thing to be with the one you love! And look, dear brother, I was right about not just you but her too! See how she has come here, to Dubai, a foreign place where she knows not a soul but you. No argument! No negotiation! She feels the pull of destiny too, just like I see it so clearly now! Ya, Allah, she may not know it, but she feels it! And that is enough for her! So I was right! And this child created from your union is the proof from Allah that I was right! Ya, Allah, our family is blessed with an heir. Kabeer, the child must be born in Bukhaara, after you are Sheikh. Oh, and the wedding. When will—"

But Kabeer had cut his sister off at that point, mumbling something about how Jenny was very focused on the restaurant and did not want to be distracted by anything. After saying he wanted it kept quiet, Kabeer had left the room, his head spinning as he wondered how the hell he was going to handle this! Not only had his sister showed a side of her that he did not know existed, but what the hell was he going to do when Yasmeena found out that Jenny had cut off any personal relationship with him?! Not to mention the fact that she wasn't pregnant!

Ya, Allah, how could I possibly make things any more complicated! My life was so simple before this curvy little American woman with her big brown eyes showed up out of nowhere! Oh, God, I want to run. I want to run far away from this. From all of it!

And so Kabeer ran. He left for Bukhaara the next day on his private jet, barricading himself in the Great Eastern Wing of the Royal Palace, spending his days and nights in a sort of trance as he wandered the empty rooms, absentmindedly stepping through the gurgling fountains where he and his brother had played.

He allowed free rein of his thoughts and memories in those weeks alone—indeed, he did not have the will to hold them back any longer. In some way it was easier to deal with the past than the present!

And it was only at the end of his self-imposed exile that those last words of his father played back to him, the soft sounds coming through on the warm breeze of a late afternoon:

"Sometimes when you think you are running away from your destiny, you are in fact running straight towards it."

Two hours later Kabeer was in Dubai, walking

through the private terminal his family kept at Dubai International Airport. He was done playing games. Done hiding from his past. Done avoiding his future.

And his future was to lead. He knew that. He had *always* known it. From the days of playing Follow the Leader as a child to the nights of leading college student protests in Paris to the afternoons in New York leading the Columbia Law Review sessions, Kabeer had always been in front, the first one there, the man everyone else looked to as an example. It was time to let the memory of Sirhan be just that—a memory, and not a chain that binds his feet to the past, preventing him from moving into the future, towards his destiny.

No more lone wolf, he decided as he slapped his cheeks like he was waking himself out of a stupor, a trance, a haze. Yes, it is time for this lone wolf to lead his pack, lead his people, lead his country, lead his family.

But first things first, he thought as he winked at his reflection, reminding himself that just because he wasn't going to be a lone wolf anymore, it didn't mean he wasn't going to be an animal when he needed to be an animal, when he wanted to be an animal, when he *craved* to be a goddamn animal!

"Sheikh Kabeer Bukhaara is in the house," he whispered in an exaggerated American accent to his reflection just as his attendant informed him the limousine was ready and waiting. "Sheikh Kabeer Bukhaara soon to be in *your* house, Jenny Jones," he said, that smile starting to emerge. "Yes, Sheikh Kabeer Bukhaara, arbiter of Allah's will on this land. And for my first act I shall make true the prophecy I have spoken." And he grinned that devilish grin full now, that wolf-smile one last time, the mischief burning in his eyes alongside the raw desire for this woman who he needed like a drug right now. "The prophecy that Jenny Jones, brown-eyed chef from Chicago, is pregnant with my child. Yes, I shall *make* it true!"

And he growled at his hazy reflection in the silver metal doors of the Jumeirah Grand's private elevators, almost laughing out loud. This woman was his. She had always been his. Allah, his sister had seen it too! Cold-hearted Yasmeena, who turned out to be a misty-eyed romantic under all that intensity!

Yes, Jenny was his, he thought as he stepped out of the elevators and three attendants came silently to his side to escort him to the waiting limousine. Jenny was his woman, and by Allah, he was her man. It did not matter how much time they had spent together in this world. That first meeting alone was worth an eternity! If that is not love, then what is love? If that is not love, then I do not care what love is—this feels so damn real, so damn true, so damn right!

But as some of that fire dissipated in the cool leather interior of his silent black BMW limousine, Kabeer knew he would have to play it cool. Despite what he felt—and what he was sure *she* felt—there was still much he had to learn about Jenny. No doubt she was focused on her restaurant, her own personal goals, her business goals. She had sounded damned well serious when she told him she wanted to keep things at a professional level, hadn't she? What if she meant it?

Ya Allah, Kabeer thought as he watched the Dubai sun blaze through the palm trees, those endless white sand dunes in the background, minarets and domes filling the space between the glass-and-steel high-rises financed by the spoils of oil money. What if she meant it?!

Ya, *Allah*, he thought again as he felt a strange desperation bubble up inside, something that made him sick, turned his stomach into knots, made him want to shout out loud, smash his fists against the dark leather walls of the limousine.

It was fear, Kabeer knew. Real fear. True vulnerability. Something Kabeer had never felt before when it came to a woman. It confused him, angered him, damned well *terrified* him! God, what if she meant what she said about "staying professional?" What can I do? This woman cannot be broken by my commands, my orders, my anger! I cannot force her to . . . to . . . to what? Love me? Force her to love me?

No, he decided as the glistening silver tower of the Burj Khalifa came into view as the limousine pulled off the highway and headed towards Jenny's restaurant space. I cannot force her to love me because there is no need to force her. All I have to do is *remind* her that she loves me. That all of this is happening *because* she loves me.

And because I love her.

And only as the limousine pulled to a silent stop outside the frosted glass windows of Jenny's restaurant, and only when Kabeer saw his woman's unmistakable silhouette through the misty glass . . . yes, only then did Kabeer realize that he had been using the word "love" like it was just a given, like it was so obvious it did not need to be analyzed, like it would be madness to assume that this was *not* love!

Ya, Allah, he thought as he stepped out of the car and straightened to full height. Swallow the fear, he told himself. Hide the vulnerability. You are Sheikh Kabeer Bukhaara and this is your queen. Relax and do not force anything. Play her game, if need be. And perhaps it is time to trust that Father's last words will apply to Jenny as well:

Just when she thinks she is running away from her destiny, she is in fact running right towards it.

20

Jenny paced the circular room so many times her head was spinning, but she couldn't sit down. It had taken an enormous amount of energy and will power to stay calm when Yasmeena revealed what Kabeer had said. She had no idea what to make of it, and in one crazy moment Jenny wondered if Kabeer actually did know she was pregnant, if he actually did have some kind of prophetic, otherworldly knowledge of the secret child within her womb!

The thought had almost floored her, but she had recovered well enough to see Yasmeena off politely and warmly, without revealing anything . . . anything about what she had decided to do.

Not having the baby had never been an option for Jenny—not because of any religious or political beliefs, but really because it just didn't feel right for her. No, the thought of having a child, the knowledge that a new life was already forming within her womb, within her private universe, a baby who would look up at her and call her Mama . . . yes, all of that sounded like a dream, a vision, something that she honestly didn't even know how to deal with yet! Not physically, and certainly not emotionally—not yet, at least.

Because now wasn't the time to deal with it, she had told herself as she prepared for that early afternoon meeting with Yasmeena. Right now you are focused on *one thing*: Your business. This is the reason you're here. Everything you want in life depends on how you navigate this final turn, she had told herself. It doesn't matter that you're hiding the baby from Kabeer, hiding the baby from the father. It may not be the most honorable thing to do, or the most fair thing to do, but hell, it's the most *sensible* thing to do!

I have to get this restaurant launched cleanly, without distractions, she told herself as she paced the circular room, touching the smooth rosewood tabletops that had just come in, the exposed brick walls that took a surprising amount of work. In six months Globe would be a success in Dubai—Jenny was sure of it. And then there was no stopping her, no stopping the expansion, no stopping Jenny Jones, MBA, from taking over the goddamn world! Or at least taking over some restaurant space in the world's most international cities. Six months. Six months of work. Six months of focus.

Six months of keeping a secret.

Perhaps she wouldn't even be really showing by then. Perhaps she could play it off by saying she couldn't keep away from her own food! Haha. Maybe her full-figured profile would actually work for her! Yes, six months.

So much could happen in six months, couldn't it? Hell, Kabeer was already seeing some Brazilian nubile, wasn't he? Perhaps Jenny would find someone as her business began to take off. Wasn't that *always* the plan? Find your own path and only then worry about finding a man to travel that path with you? Don't get derailed. This is complicated, yes. But you can handle it. Six months. Be a goddamn professional for six months, and deal with it later. Deal with *him* later!

Him. Kabeer Bukhaara.

She watched in a sort of panic, a kind of haze, a little bit of a daze as a black stretch limousine stopped outside her restaurant. It wasn't a complete surprise, but Jenny could feel her stomach twist with a sudden tension, and ohgod it felt . . . it felt . . . it felt . . .

Oh, grow up, she told herself. So you haven't been in a room with Kabeer in almost a month. Seeing him is going to have an impact emotionally, and that's fine. It's natural. It doesn't mean anything. It's only normal to have a reaction to a man with whom you've shared an intimate moment. Heck, if that guy Steve walked in here—the guy I almost slept with over a year ago—I'd probably have some kind of reaction. And so would he. We're human, after all. It's normal! So accept it, push it aside, and get down to business. He's just a guy.

Sheikh Kabeer Bukhaara walked in right then, tall and handsome, his jaw set, that half-smile on his lips, head slightly cocked like seeing Jenny was the easiest thing in the world for him, like *everything* was the easiest thing in the world for him. He wore a blue silk shirt, impeccably tailored, top two buttons lazily undone. He had lost some of his natural tan, though he had clearly still been working out, if not going out in the sun much. And there was a strange new confidence, perhaps even a calmness—real or calculated, Jenny couldn't tell yet—in his eyes as he glanced quickly around the restaurant and finally settled his gaze on the open kitchen towards the back of the restaurant.

"Magnificent," he said, walking right past Jenny without so much as a hello as she took a quick breath when he smelled his familiar musk, that unique masculine aroma of his that seemed to touch something deep inside, so deep that it couldn't possibly have been put there by that one day a month ago! "This is Michelin Star quality," Kabeer said, knocking on the countertop of the open kitchen, checking the Italian wood cabinets." I like the semi-circular cut of the stainless steel counter, the way it hugs the back of the space. And this long bar facing the open kitchen is the chef's table, is it not? Six seats only. Very nice. Intimate, isn't it? One can actually have a conversation with the real food-lovers. We are going to have a wood top placed on this countertop, right? Fixed to the stainless steel? Dark wood and shining steel offset each other wonderfully."

Jenny blinked as she took all of it in. Kabeer seemed so cool, so confident, so . . . so professional! Sure, that swagger and cockiness was still up front and center, but there was a genuine excitement in the way he talked about the kitchen, the design, the environment. Yes, he was clearly excited to see the space. But he had barely said two words to *her*! No hello even! Certainly no hug. Not even a handshake!

Now she was almost angry as she watched Kabeer walk around the restaurant like he owned the god-damn place. She still couldn't get her head around the lie he had told Yasmeena, couldn't understand the why, the how, the what, and the WTF!?

"Oh, do not tell me you have prepared some food!" Kabeer called out from behind the chef's counter, just inside the open kitchen. He stood in front of the six-foot tall stack of glass-fronted ovens, his hands on his hips, back to Jenny.

The three dishes she had prepared earlier for Yasmeena to sample were in there keeping warm, and Jenny suddenly snapped out of her confusion and walked briskly to the kitchen, not so much as a glance at Kabeer as he stood there, his back still to her. Jenny welcomed the aroma of food as she pulled open the oven doors, glad that she was able to control her reaction to the aroma of *him*!

"Little-Vietnam Roast Duck," she announced, sliding out the first tray.

"South Side Organic Meatloaf," she proclaimed as the second tray emerged.

"Devon Street Green-and-Yellow Chicken," she called out in excitement as she presented the third entrée. "Gotta have some Chicago in there!"

She arranged the items on three pristine white plates and placed them on a serving cart, slowly wheeling the cart to that round table as Kabeer turned his attention to the dishes and then, finally, to her. Jenny thought she saw a flash of something in Kabeer's eyes as he made eye contact—something beneath that coolly professional, supremely confident, casually cold persona that Jenny had always suspected wasn't the whole story.

What do I see in those green eyes, she thought as she pushed the cart past him slowly, breaking eye contact and exhaling hard as she turned her back. What did I see, Kabeer? Did I see you actually *flinch* when you looked at me? Was that a flash of . . . of . . . hesitation, vulnerability, *fear* in your eyes when you saw how professional I can be around you, when you saw that I'm not going to run into your strong arms, fall victim to that green-eyed gaze, melt from your smooth, Arabian accent, swoon from the way you smell, the way you talk, the way you . . . the way you are!

And now Jenny was glad Kabeer couldn't see *her* face, because she wasn't sure what he'd see in her big brown eyes, read in her expression, sense in her as she felt her body react to Kabeer's presence, react in the same way it had the first time they met, that otherworldly connection that just didn't make logical sense given how little time they had spent together.

Oh, God, I'm carrying this man's child and he doesn't know, Jenny thought as a mixture of shame and panic ripped through her. For a moment she longed to just push this food cart aside and run to his arms and say, "Kabeer, I'm pregnant with your child! With *our* child! I didn't want it to happen but it did! And now that it's happened I want it so badly! And maybe I want *you* so badly too!"

But she stayed quiet, brought the professional smile back to her rosy red lips, and made sure her hands weren't shaking as she began to place the hot dishes on the round table.

"That looks incredible," Kabeer said from behind her, and Jenny felt his eyes on her just like she felt his heat so close, a heat that was making *her* heat rise in that annoying, unstoppable way that had gotten her into this damned mess to begin with!

Now Kabeer was right behind her, *so* damned close, and hell this was *not* professional, and God he was lightly touching her arms as she placed the second heavy dish on the table, and his touch was so light, right there, like he was saying, "I am right here, Jenny. Right behind you. Just like I was on that stairway leading to the boat. Right behind you, always. Whether you like it or not. Whether you know it or not. Whether you will have it or not."

"It smells magnificent, Jenny," Kabeer said now, softly, carefully, and she felt his warm, fresh breath in her hair as he spoke. "Tell me what is what."

"Little-Vietnam Roast Duck," Jenny said softly, her voice wavering at first. But then she found her focus and cleared her throat and spoke loudly. "Inspired by the street cuisine you get during summer in Chicago's Little Vietnam."

"Wonderful," Kabeer said, drawing back and walking around the table. He stopped at a chair across from her, his gaze on Jenny, not the food. He held the look for a long time, and when Jenny kept her focus on the food, he took an impatient breath, waited a moment, and then seemed to regain his own focus. "And this is the American meatloaf?" he said in a tone that was almost too loud, that seemed to betray some of the tension within this cool, calm, confident Sheikh. "The Arabs will go mad for it here!"

Jenny nodded as she smiled inside. "South Side Organic Meatloaf. The look and feel of meatloaf that's standard fare in the lower income homes of Chicago's South Side, but instead of spam and ground-beef, I use organic grains, vegetables, and local, humanely treated, naturally-raised beef and chicken. No pork, of course. It's shockingly good."

"This last one smells Indian," Kabeer said, finally seeming to turn his attention to the food as he pointed at the third dish. "Oh, correct. Devon Street is the heart of the Indian part of Chicago." He reached out with his finger to try a bit of the sauce, but Jenny smacked his hand *hard* with a wooden serving spoon.

"Manners," she said without looking at him. "We're going to be sharing each dish."

Kabeer shrugged, sucking his finger and looking up at her. "I did not think anyone here would have a problem sharing my germs," he said without hesitation. Now he looked around the table, glanced over the empty restaurant, and gazed up at her with that schoolboyish, wide-eyed stare of innocence and wonder. "Oh, Allah. There is no one else here! Just the two of us. You and me. Kabeer and Jenny." Now the playfulness in his voice was gone, and there was a depth in his words, a resonance in his language, a hint of something deep, old, and real in what he said. "Just you and me. Man and woman. Kabeer and Jenny. The Sheikh and his Queen."

Jenny felt a silence descend upon the table—a crushing, heavy silence during which the sound of her heartbeat hit heavy in her eardrums. The blood was pounding, her temples throbbing. She wasn't sure she had heard right. She wasn't sure if Kabeer had said what he said. She felt dizzy and weak. Her heart leapt one moment, almost stopped beating the next. She was hot beneath her open hair, cold as the shivers ran down her back beneath her thin satin blouse. She wasn't sure if she wanted to slap Kabeer or kiss him. Stop. Stop. *Stop*!

Perhaps the hesitation served her, because she was so shocked, so taken aback, so not sure what to say that she simply said nothing. She sat down across from Kabeer like she was in a dream again, and for the next minute or so she focused on carefully serving each of them a little of each dish, making sure not to let the items mix on the individual plates.

Just sit and don't look him in the eye, she told herself. Focus on the food. Chew mindfully. And if that doesn't work, think about something totally different. Count sheep if you have to!

Kabeer took a long look at her, but did not say anything else. He waited for another long moment, waited for Jenny to look him in the eye. She did not. Finally Kabeer took a breath and silently leaned back in his chair, his expression hard, his jaw set, his eyes burning with green fire as he seemed to be forcing himself to hold his words back, perhaps hold *himself* back.

The Sheikh waited for Jenny to begin eating. Then he bowed his head and began. The two of them chewed quietly in an air of silence so heavy, so thick, so tangible that it could have been served as the fourth dish on the small round table, and it took all Jenny's will to stay focused on the food and avoid looking directly at the Sheikh.

The silence lasted so long that Jenny felt she might explode, and then, in a bright, cheerful voice that cut through the tension, Kabeer said, "The duck: a hint of cranberry in the marinade. Meatloaf: infused with raw ginger and garlic *after* it is done cooking, which is why the flavor is fresh and strong. Chicken: a touch of horseradish in the sauce—*very* unusual for Indian food." He flashed her his cocky grin and then wiped his mouth, leaned back, and took a sip of water. "How am I doing?"

Jenny blinked like she was hyperventilating with her eyelids. She was sure her face was bright red, and she forced herself to stay seated and not say something she couldn't take back. She thought for a moment, then matched his smile with one of her own. "Raspberry, not cranberry. Lemongrass, not ginger. And just plain ol' mustard, not horseradish."

"Close," Kabeer said.

"Close doesn't cut it."

"Missed by an inch."

"Might as well have missed by a mile."

"I do not think I missed."

"You calling me a liar?"

Kabeer shrugged. "I know the different between raspberry and cranberry."

"It's raspberry reduction. Picks up some sweetness as it breaks down."

"Raspberry reduction would not hold up so evenly. It falls apart at the temperature you need to roast the duck."

"Oh?" Jenny raised an eyebrow, and although she hated it, she could feel a *real* smile teasing its way onto her lips. "And what temperature is that?"

Kabeer held her gaze for a long, cool moment. "The skin is roasted to crisp perfection while the inside is moist and just the right side of cooked. So I'd say *insanely* high heat and then you turned off the oven and let it cook in the afterglow."

"Afterglow?" Jenny could feel the heat rise in her cheeks. "Is that a technical term?"

"It is *absolutely* a technical term!"

And suddenly they were smiling, chatting, laughing, *flirting* . . . Kabeer teasing her as Jenny giggled, the two of them verbally pushing and pulling as they ate and drank, Kabeer snagging a piece of duck from her plate as she tried to playfully stop him, and they were playing like children, chatting like old friends, laughing like . . . like . . . like lovers?

Love?

Was it even possible to bring that four-letter word into this? How could love happen like this? It took months, perhaps years to get to know someone, didn't it? Love doesn't just happen, does it? You can't just start off by being in love, can you? Can you? Can't you? Aren't you? Won't you? Don't you? Do you? Does he? Does he? Does he?! *Stop!*

"Your sister was here," Jenny said suddenly, smiling as she looked down at her plate and then up at Kabeer. "We talked for a while."

Kabeer looked like he had indigestion for a moment, and Jenny couldn't help but feel a strange sort of victory right then, an odd sort of power, like she was, for at least one damn moment, in control of this madness that her life had become!

His eyes narrowed now, and Jenny knew he was trying to figure out what Yasmeena had said to her. Clearly Yasmeena hadn't talked to him after leaving the restaurant, and so Jenny kept going, starting to enjoy this in a way. "She's very different, you know."

Kabeer exhaled. "Different from me? That is an understatement."

Jenny shrugged. "I meant she's different from what I thought she was." She touched her hair unconsciously, glancing directly at Kabeer now. "As far as different from you . . . not as different as I thought. Maybe not as different as *you* thought." Now she shifted in her chair and looked down for a moment. 'I mean, not like I know either of you that well. I'm just—"

"I think you know me *very* well, Jenny," Kabeer said, leaning forward, reaching out, grabbing her by the wrist. His grip tightened on her wrist now, and she could feel him pull—gently, but unremittingly, with no give, no slack. "Listen, Jenny, this story with that model Selena—it is fake. Planted. Nothing has happened between us."

"Why not?" Jenny said, the words coming so quickly she almost choked. She looked at Kabeer's fingers around her wrist but made no overt move to break free. "Not your type?"

Kabeer let go instantly and leaned back. His jaw tightened and it looked like he was literally biting his tongue right then. A smile emerged now, that "planted" smile that Jenny recognized from every posed tabloid picture of him back in Chicago. "Oh, she is certainly my type. You have seen a photograph of her? Very sexy. And I did not say nothing is *going* to happen between us. I just said nothing has happened *yet*."

"And I said why not?" Jenny said, crossing her arms over her chest now, leaning back and staring at him, her mouth firm, her look defiant.

"You know why not!" Kabeer growled, reaching for her hand across the table again.

But Jenny pushed her chair back from the table, away from him. "Stop it, Kabeer. I—"

"No, *you* stop it, Jenny! You cannot play this game at my level and expect to win. There is something between us—something real, something I cannot explain, something I thought meant nothing but now I know means something, means *everything*! It sounds mad, I know, but I am Sheikh and you are my queen. That is the only thing that makes sense to me. That is the only way to explain why I feel like this, why *you* feel like this! I know it and you know it. You want to fight it and keep your distance—fine. You want me to keep things *professional* while you get the restaurant up—OK. Just don't try to convince me— or yourself—that there is nothing here."

Kabeer stood up now with a force that shook the heavy wooden table, sending silverware clattering to the tiles, half-filled glasses shaking in his wake. He walked to where Jenny sat on that straight-backed wooden chair that was pushed back away from the table.

Kabeer stood before her, towering above Jenny as his body hardened, his voice deeper but somehow soft, intense but warm, harsh but still delicate. He looked down into her eyes, and this time she could not look away. "I do not know what my sister told you, but it does not matter. Yes, because now, now that I am near you again, looking into those big brown eyes that have haunted my goddamn dreams for the past month . . . yes, now I know why I lied to my sister." He smiled now, looking up at the ceiling and then down into her eyes again. "Because it was not a lie, in some sense. It was not a lie because I finally understand what destiny means, what 'meant-to-be' means, what . . . what . . . what love means."

Jenny felt a tremendous, unconscious swell in her deepest core as he spoke, and her lower lip trembled as she looked into the Sheikh's eyes. She couldn't trust herself to speak, but speak she did, the words coming out like it was someone else talking:

"But Kabeer," she mumbled, realizing that she didn't believe what she herself was saying, realizing that she already knew the answer to her unspoken question. "But Kabeer, it's only been two months! How can it be love? How can it be—"

"How can it *not* be love?!" Kabeer bellowed, and now he was on his knees, his head down near hers, his eyes locked with hers, his presence enveloping her, drawing her in, opening her up though she *desperately* wanted to stay closed, to hold her ground, stick with her goddamn plan . . . that plan which seemed so hopelessly futile now that she was near him, near Kabeer, near her man, the father of the child within her. "How can it not be love, little Jenny? How can it not?" Kabeer whispered, leaning in close, so close now, so damned close . . .

Oh, God, I have to tell him, the voice inside her shrieked as he drew near. I have to tell him, I have to tell him, I have to tell him!

But then the voice was lost because he kissed her, kissed her hard, kissed her deep, kissed her in a way that made it so clear that time meant nothing when it came to matters of love, that lovers can live a lifetime in an afternoon, an eternity in a moment.

21

And the moment to tell him had passed, and now the only words that came from her mouth were "Oh, *God*, Kabeer," the sound coming out with throttled urgency, her eyes meeting his gaze as she felt him pull her by the wrists, pull her hard, dragging her to her feet like he couldn't control himself, like he had controlled himself too damned long.

He leaned in for a fierce, raw kiss that she was sure would leave a bruise, and before she had a chance to catch her breath, he had her by the back of the neck and he pulled her swiftly to him as his fingers gripped her hair by the roots.

"Kabeer," she muttered, her words sounding muffled as he smothered her lips with his, pulling her hair with one hand as his other hand closed *hard* on her right breast. "The door, Kabeer. It's not—"

"I do not give a damn, Jenny," he growled as he licked her neck hungrily. "I do not give a *damn*!"

And he stood and broke off the kiss, grabbing her by the waist, lifting her *clean* off her feet as he backed up into that heavy round table, his hard body colliding with it, forks and knives clattering to the floor, sideplates and waterglasses shattering on the tiles. The Sheikh dragged her now as she swooned, dizzy from his violent, pent-up passion, breathless from her own spiraling heat, dragged her across the smooth tiles to that open kitchen, one hand feverishly unbuttoning her blouse, holding her body secure in his strong arms, holding her from behind and moving her with a power that was as gentle as it was urgent. Jenny stumbled out of her heels, her soft cheeks hitting Kabeer's rock-hard chest as he lifted her once more and effortlessly popped her up on that steel kitchen countertop like she was that feather in the breeze again, that wisp of smoke in the endless night.

"I have thought about you every day when we were apart, Jenny," he muttered against her face as he kissed her *hard*, pulling, kneading, massaging her full breasts beneath that thin satin blouse, his strong fingers sliding down her tight bra-cups, finding her stiff nipples and pinching with *desperation*, rubbing her hips through her jeans, feverishly pushing his hands between her ample thighs. "Every damned day, you hear? It has never been this way for me, not with any woman. And it can never be this way with any other woman, I am sure of it." Now he pulled away for just one moment, but it was one of those moments that last an eternity, because he looked deep into her brown eyes and said:

"Do not ask how this can be love, Jenny. The only question is how can this be anything *but* love! It can *only* be love, Jenny. It can *only* be love!"

And he kissed her again as the hot kitchen lights blazed down on the two lovers, and Jenny gurgled and gasped, flailed and fluttered, shook and shivered as she felt herself surrender to the Sheikh, surrender to his passion, his need, his desire. His love.

Surrender to his love.

22

She wore blue jeans that were snug around her curves in a way that had gotten him hard the moment he saw her turn and walk toward the kitchen. From that moment on Kabeer knew he wasn't leaving this restaurant until those jeans were a crumpled heap on the unfinished floor, her bra and panties swinging from the old-style ceiling fans, the smell of sex infused into every nook and crevasse of this half-finished space.

Now she was sitting up on that broad, sturdy steel counter facing him, her thin top already half-unbuttoned. He could see the swell of her breasts, and as he brought his face close he felt the heat of her body released through the open buttons of her shirt.

"Every goddamn day, Jenny," he rumbled as he pushed his face between her breasts, his tongue darting into her cleavage, licking left and then right as he *ripped* the last two buttons off her shirt and tore it off her back. "The way you looked when you were lying under me as that boat rocked and rolled on the waves. The way your black bra was pushed up over your magnificent breasts. Ya, Allah, Jenny. I could barely contain myself then, and I cannot, I WILL not, contain myself now!"

"Don't you dare contain yourself," she whispered into him, her breath feeling hot and urgent against his skin. "Oh, God, don't you *dare*, Kabeer!"

Now the Sheikh pulled back, a smile of ecstasy lighting up his dark face. He looked at his woman, little curvy Jenny perched up on that broad countertop, those big brown eyes staring up at him, her soft white skin looking lush and fresh under the hot lights, her breasts looking gorgeous and full, the top-down view of her womanly hips and thighs getting him so hot, so hard, so goddamn *wild*!

He played with her breasts as he kissed her deep, kneading the flesh with his palms, teasing her nipples between his fingers, pinching gently at first, now harder, pulling, plucking, kissing, and suddenly *slapping* her soft breasts as she *squealed* in surprise, her eyes going wide as she inhaled sharply.

"Kabeer!" she shouted. "Oh, my *God*, Kabeer!"

"*Baladi alihat, biludi alhabiba, ya mulkatan!*" he muttered as he reached around and expertly popped the bra-clasp, grinning down at her as the bra-cups fell loose from her swollen breasts. "My queen. Ya, Allah, my *queen*!"

Jenny's eyes went wide again for a moment as he uttered the words, her eyelids fluttering as he kissed her face, fondled her breasts, his fingers making her tremble. She kissed him back, and he could damn well *taste* her arousal. This is right, he thought. Allah, this is right.

He pressed her thick thighs through her jeans again, squeezing with all his strength, pressing hard until he could feel it in the way she was breathing into his mouth—those short little gasps that she had produced the first time he made her come.

"My queen," he said again, the words coming out slurred as they kissed frantically. "I feel it. I see it. I know it. You are woman to my man. Just as you will be Queen to my Sheikh. Just like you will be mother to my child. Yes, mother to my child, Jenny!"

She jerked in his arms as he said it, and he shuddered as his arousal took him close to delirium. Ya, Allah, she feels it too! I may have lied about it, but it is truly a prophecy! A prophecy that I will make true right now, right here, as Allah blesses us, as eternity watches us! I will *make* it true!

"I should have told you," Jenny mumbled as she broke off the kiss to take a desperate breath of air.

"Oh, God, I should have told you, Kabeer. You had a right to know. I should have told—"

"Told me what?" Kabeer said, as her words finally registered in his overheated brain. "That you know this is love? That you know that our bodies cannot lie? That what we feel is love and cannot be anything else, no matter what logic and common sense and—"

"No," she gasped as she came up for air again, her hands clawing at his hair as he unbuttoned her jeans, feeling the warmth of her sex on his fingers as he touched the front of her soaked panties. "That I'm pregnant, Kabeer. That I'm really pregnant."

The blood of arousal was surging so hard through Kabeer's veins that he could barely hear anything as his head buzzed, his heart pounded, his hardness throbbed as he pushed his hand down the front of her panties and ran his stiff fingers along her wetness, finding her warm slit, now sliding his fingers inside as she moaned and tensed up around his flexed arm. Her words sounded faint and faraway as his hunger rose along with her moans, but slowly they came into focus, came into view like solid objects spinning through a dream.

What did she say?

What . . . did . . . she . . . say . . . ?

What . . . did . . . she . . .

And now Kabeer was falling into an abyss in that dream, and it was he that was spinning, his body twisting and turning, his mind spinning and slamming, and he could not breathe, could not see, could not talk, could not . . . could not . . . could not *believe* . . .

. . . could not believe she had kept this from him! Kept it from *him*! She did not trust her feelings about me? She did not trust my feelings about her? She did not trust *me*?!

It took all his will, all his strength, all his goddamn power to bring himself back under control, to still his mind, harness his anger, quell his rage, roll back his arousal. Yes, it took all his strength, the strength of a king, the strength of a Sheikh, the strength of his ancestors even . . . but he did it, and suddenly there was calm, there was focus, there was control, and Kabeer buried his passion, barricaded his desire, denied his need, and with a cold smile that he could see shook her to the core, the Sheikh *grabbed* Jenny by the hair, pulled her head back, kissed her *hard* on the mouth, and finally locked his eyes onto hers, his gaze speaking a thousand words, his words spinning a thousand nightmares.

"I cannot have a queen who does not trust her king," he whispered. "I cannot."

And he let go of her hair, turned, and walked away.

23

She *screamed* as the door swung shut, the wood and metal doorframe making a tinny sound that made her want to scream again. She wasn't sure if she was angry with him or herself. But it wasn't just anger. It wasn't just frustration at being left in this state. No, it was because she knew Kabeer was right. She hadn't trusted him. Even worse, she hadn't trusted *herself*!

Oh, God, Kabeer was right! She *knew* it was love the moment he first touched her, didn't she? It didn't make sense, but since when does love *need* to make sense?! Did it make sense that she was here in the United Arab Emirates, accepting the change of location without argument?! Did it make sense that *so* much happened *so* quick and *all* of it seemed so damned natural, so damned perfect, so damned . . . so damned *wonderful*!?

In all that focus, all that perseverance, all that dedication to the dream of her own business, being self-sufficient, making her mark on the world, did she deny herself the right to chase that other dream alongside? That ancient dream of knowing love, knowing marriage, knowing motherhood? That dream of having a man she desired, a man she trusted, a man who trusted *her*?!

Because wasn't that what Kabeer had shown in every damn thing he did? That he *trusted* her? From the very first act of taking her to the boat, introducing her to his family, in his own way telling them that this woman, Jennifer Bethany Jones, was different, was special, was . . . was *his*! Perhaps he didn't know it at the time. Certainly she didn't know it at the time. But that doesn't mean it wasn't true! It was true! *He* was true! Their *love* was true! The only thing that wasn't true was Jenny: She wasn't being true to herself, to her *entire* self, to the fullness of what it meant to be a woman, a woman in love with herself, in love with her work, in love with her *man*!

And Jenny the woman, the complete woman, just sat there shaking and wet, sweat beading on her forehead, the smell of perspiration and the aroma of her sex heavy in the air. Her shirt was in tatters on the counter behind her. She didn't even know where her bra was. Her panties were soaked, jeans damp at the crotch. She could taste him on her lips, smell him with every breath, see him when she closed her eyes to blink. She cursed out loud and spat on the floor and cursed again. Then she slowly reached for that torn shirt and tried in vain to do something with it.

"There's no way," she said out loud, shaking her head, almost in tears simply because her body and mind were in overload. "There's no way I can do this. I'll screw up everything if I have to work with him. There's no way. Absolutely not. What was I thinking?"

She muttered to herself now as she paced, that tattered blouse hanging off her as she tried to pull it close. The Sheikh's words hung heavy in the air: *All* his words.

"Woman to my man . . ."

"Mother to my child . . ."

"Queen to my Sheikh . . ."

Queen to his Sheikh. Queen to his Sheikh. Queen to his Sheikh.

The words began to echo in her head now, the sounds so loud and real that Jenny worried that she was truly going insane, seriously losing her mind, completely falling apart.

Queen to his Sheikh. Queen . . . queen . . . queen . . .

And as she paced in her delirium, stumbled in her

hysteria, blinked through her confusion, she got that strange, eerie, otherworldly feeling she had first gotten when she stood there on that deck, stood before the entire Royal Family of Bukhaara, stood there with her back straight, her shoulders back, her chin pointed up. Yes, she had stood there proud, stood there strong, stood there in spite of her fear, in defiance of her self-consciousness . . . stood there and showed them that she was indeed one of them, that though on the surface she was plain old Jenny Jones from Illinois, the blood that flowed through her veins was as regal as anyone else's on that boat.

Yes, she thought as the images and emotions bubbled up from depths that felt profoundly strong, unfathomably ancient, indescribably real . . . oh, God, yes.

I am that queen, aren't I? I am that queen.

"I am that queen," came the whisper, curling its way from those depths of her soul like how an ancient river winds its way to the ocean. Her voice sounded thick, full, strong in a way that startled her. And now Jenny felt her body straighten up, her shoulders pull themselves back as if supported by the grace of the gods, her chin point to the heavens as she felt a smile break through the distress, calm break through the storm, strength smash through that moment of powerlessness.

"I am that queen," she said to the circular room,

the tables and chairs bearing silent witness as the fingers of the universe placed an invisible crown atop the round head of Jenny Jones. "And I am *his* queen . *His* queen. *His* queen!"

"I am, I am, I am!" she sobbed as she stood there proudly, her smile so wide now that it damn well hurt! "I am, I am, I *am*!"

And as Queen Jenny stood there in the center of her court, the front door burst open in what felt like an explosion of stardust, and Sheikh Kabeer Bukhaara roared his way into the room, his face peaked with emotion, his eyes like emeralds ablaze, everything about him asking her the question that she was already answering:

Will you? Are you? Do you?

I will. I am. I do.

I do.

24

And they made love, right then and there, like man and woman, like animals and gods, like husband and wife, like king and queen. And as their shared climax roared in like that ancient river breaking on the shores of forever, shaking the very foundations of the mighty Burj Khalifa that towered about them in the desert sun, Eternity herself smiled down upon the lovers and recorded the moment for all time.

And in that everlasting moment, beneath her fluttering eyelids Jenny saw the future, saw her future, their future, the universe's future . . .

She saw Kabeer being crowned Sheikh, Queen Jenny by his side, her curves accentuated by the world's most beautiful baby bump, a ring the size of Jupiter on her finger . . . and she saw herself launching her restaurants, on her own, as head chef, letting the food speak for itself like she had always wanted, and the reviews were rolling in, praise and adulation, success and expansion . . . Dubai . . . Sydney . . . Moscow . . . Vienna . . . Tokyo . . . Paris . . . New York . . . London . . . Chicago . . . and everything fused together and spun apart as Jenny *howled* in the Sheikh's arms . . . and now she saw their child running through the streets of old Bukhaara as she and Kabeer followed, Queen Jenny pregnant once more, all of them laughing, the domes and minarets laughing with them under the desert sun, the golden sand dunes sparkling like hillocks made of stardust, and for a moment everything seemed insane, overwhelming, impossible as Jenny *wailed* through that endless orgasm as the Sheikh drove deep within her, and she wondered how she could do all of it, how she could be all of it, how she could live all of it . . .

And through all of the ecstasy and chaos, the madness and passion, the dreams and desires . . . yes, at the end of it all, just like at the beginning of it all, Jenny Jones heard that whisper come through so soft yet so clear . . .

Jump in, little Jenny.

Jump in.

∞

FROM ANNABELLE WINTERS

Thanks for reading.

Join my private list at **annabellewinters.com/join** to get steamy epilogues, exclusive scenes with side characters, and a chance to join my advance review team.

And do write to me at **mail@annabellewinters.com** anytime. I really like hearing from you.

Love,
Anna.

Printed in Dunstable, United Kingdom